THE LEGACY OF THE NURUS

CHRONICLES OF THE NURU ASCENSION

NIE HARVEY

FEARLESS REIGN PRESS

Published in the United States by Fearless Reign Press, an imprint of MPowering Legacy Publishing, a division of MPowering Legacy, LLC, Mississippi.

www.fearlessreignpress.com

The Legacy of the Nurus

Book One: Chronicles of the Nuru Ascension

Ebook ISBN: 979-8-9991740-1-7

Print ISBN: 979-8-9991740-0-0

Manufactured in the United States of America.

Printed in the United States of America

CONTENTS

DEDICATION

To my firstborn, Sedric Tayari—your unique way of seeing the world, your "blindisms," and your joyful spirit guided me back to the realms of fantasy and science fiction. The simple flick of your hands rekindled my imagination and reminded me of the wonder within the supernatural.

I also dedicate this book to Black women, whose magic is ancestral, powerful, and often coveted. You are extraordinary. Never doubt what you are capable of.

THE LEGACY OF THE NURUS

OFFICIAL SOUNDTRACK COMPANION

Book Soundtrack Cues
This novel uses Book Soundtrack Cues—footnotes that cue specific songs from the official soundtrack. When you see a cue, press play for a fully immersive, cinematic reading experience. You can access the full soundtrack **here***.*

Prologue. "Glory" – Common & John Legend

Chapter One: "Way Down We Go" – KALEO

Chapter Two: "Is You Krazy" – Lady London

Chapter Three: "DNA." – Kendrick Lamar

Chapter Four: "The Hills" – The Weeknd

Chapter Five: "Mask off" – Future

Chapter Six: "I'll Find You" – Lecrae ft. Tori Kelly

Chapter Seven: "Spirit" – Beyoncé

Chapter Eight: "Rise Up" – Andra Day

Chapter Nine: "Essence" – Tems

Chapter Ten: "The King's Affirmation" – Iniko

Chapter Eleven: "Not Afraid" – Eminem

Chapter Twelve: "Let the Beat Build" – Lil Wayne

Chapter Thirteen: "Power" – Kanye West ft. Dwele

Chapter Fourteen: "Run This Town" – Jay-Z, Rihanna, Kanye West

Chapter Fifteen: "Glory and Gore" – Lorde

Chapter Sixteen: "Radioactive" – Imagine Dragons

Chapter Seventeen: "Drop the World" – Lil Wayne ft. Eminem

Chapter Eighteen: "Pretty Little Birds" – SZA ft. Isaiah Rashad

Chapter Nineteen: "Sandcastles" – Beyoncé

Chapter Twenty: "We Gon' Be Alright" – Tye Tribbett

Chapter Twenty-One: "Rescue" – Lauren Daigle

Chapter Twenty-Two: "Free Mind" – Tems

Chapter Twenty-Three: "Warriors Imagine" – Dragons

SYNOPSIS

Pia Pierce thought she was just a college student with big dreams and a simple life in a small town in Mississippi. But when bullets miss, time slows, and a mysterious green light shields her from danger, she begins to question everything—her town, her family, even herself.

Uncovering secrets buried deep in her Southern bloodline, Pia learns she's descended from the Nurus—children of divine beings tasked with protecting the world from darkness. With the help of her long-lost great-great-grandmother, Pia must master her powers, confront her family's legacy, and navigate a town teetering between shadow and salvation while evading bigger threats.

Because the storm isn't coming.

It's already here.

PROLOGUE

"*D* *amn niggers! When I find you, I'll kill you dead!*" Beaumont's voice cut through the thick Mississippi night, laced with rage and whiskey.

Israel Webster kept moving, his breath heavy, muscles burning. His wife, Perlie, slumped against his back, arms wrapped tight around his shoulders as he and his brother, Jonah, carried her through the dense woods.

Perlie was nine and a half months pregnant. That baby was coming whether or not they had time for it.[1]

But stopping meant death.

The Beaumonts were after them—Beaumont and his boys, Rufus and Adam. They'd set fire to the Webster home when they refused to sell their land, thinking they'd smoke them out. But Jonah had

---

1. **Book Soundtrack Cue**: "Glory" – Common & John Legend.

caught wind of their plan hours before, and the brothers were ready.

"You holdin' on, baby?" Israel whispered to Perlie, adjusting his grip beneath her thighs.

She nodded weakly, sweat slicking her brow. "Mmhm...but, Izzy. ..I can't hold this baby much longer."

Israel's jaw tightened. They needed a place to hide. Now.

"Over there," Jonah whispered, nodding toward a dip in the earth ahead. "That's the spot I been working on. We can hold up there 'til they pass."

It was a ten-by-ten dugout, hidden beneath a thicket of twigs and branches. Not much, but enough.

Jonah dropped down first, reaching up to help Israel ease Perlie into the space. She groaned, her belly tightening beneath his hands.

Israel kissed her forehead. "We got a good head start. You doin' good, baby."

Perlie's breath hitched. Tears welled in her eyes. "Izzy... this baby comin' now."

Jonah, steady as ever, wiped sweat from his brow. "Alright then," he said, voice calm. "Israel, pass me that towel in the corner. We got everything we need to bring my niece into this world."

They moved fast. Israel laid Perlie down as Jonah pulled out his knife, boiled clean in a small tin pot hours before.

"Alright, Perlie," Jonah murmured, positioning himself at her feet. "I need you to breathe through it. Ain't much room, but I made sure it's enough for you to push. We gon' be alright."

Perlie clenched Israel's hand, biting back a moan as she pushed. Her whole body trembled, the pain rippling through her like waves.

"That's it," Jonah urged. "One more, now. You almost there."

Then—

"I think they went this way," Adam's voice rang out, too damn close.

Israel froze. His grip on Perlie tightened as his pulse thundered in his ears.

They were right above them.

Rufus' boots crunched against fallen twigs. "Ain't nowhere else for 'em to run," he sneered. "Betcha that nigger woman done dropped her mutt right here in these woods."

Perlie clenched her jaw, rocking her newborn against her chest, willing her to stay quiet.

Then—Rhema cried.

The sound was tiny—a soft, newborn wail—but in the heavy silence of the woods, it may as well have been a gunshot.

Rufus stopped walking.

"Y'all hear that?" Beaumont's voice was sharp with wicked amusement. "Sounds like a fresh lil' pickaninny just took her first breath."

Jonah's hands shook as he cut the umbilical cord, wrapping Rhema in the towel. Perlie sobbed, pressing frantic kisses to her baby's face.

"Shh, shhh, baby girl, please..."

Too late.

"They're down here!" Rufus hollered.

The wooden planks above ripped away, and suddenly, they were staring up into the double barrels of Beaumont's shotgun.

Jonah threw himself in front of them.

Israel tightened his arms around Perlie and Rhema, chest heaving.

This was it.

Beaumont sneered down at them, cocking the gun. "Told y'all I was gon' kill you dead."

The night air shifted.

Something ancient stirred.

And then—

Rhema stopped crying.

She blinked up at Beaumont, wide-eyed, a small crease forming between her tiny brows.

Her eyes—

They shimmered.

A green glow flickered behind her irises, faint but undeniable.

Jonah's breath caught.

Israel's grip tightened.

Beaumont faltered, just for a second—just long enough.

Click-click.

Pow... pow.

CHAPTER ONE

The car rolled to a stop. No one was around; no cars passed by. No voices. No movement. Just her and the old Honda Accord that made sure she got to her destinations until now. The empty stretch of road and the moon kept quiet company.

Pia gripped the steering wheel, heart pounding. The front right tire had gone flat barely a hundred yards from the exit—too far to walk alone this late at night. Her phone was dead, and she wasn't about to wander into the dark hoping for a good Samaritan. Not in Windsorville. Not with the way crime had jumped lately.[1]

She exhaled, scanning her surroundings. The glow of a gas station sign flickered in the distance, hazy against the night. If she could make it there, she could call her dad. But stepping out alone? That was a gamble she wasn't sure she wanted to take.

---

1. **Book Soundtrack Cue**: "Way Down We Go" – KALEO.

It was a little after 10 p.m. and her phone was dead. With the increase in random shootings, car jackings, and gang violence, Pia did not want to risk being a victim on the 6 o'clock news in the morning.

Pia was a petite girl in her late teens, but the veins emerging from her hands and legs showed that she was athletic. She was a college student, level-headed, and focused on her goal of being a dance teacher. She didn't have much in life, but what she did have was all she needed.

She muttered a low prayer, a habit ingrained since childhood. *"Lord, cover me. Keep me safe."* Then, as if channeling her father, she added under her breath, *"Ain't no sense in panickin'. Think first, move second."*

Just as she debated her next move, three hard knocks rattled the passenger window.

Pia's breath caught.

A man stood just outside, his face partially obscured by the shadow of her dim headlights. His clothes were dirty, worn through at the elbows, and his unkempt beard stretched down his neck. He leaned in slightly, eyes searching hers through the glass.

"You need help?" His voice was raspy but not unkind. "I can walk you to a phone."

Pia didn't answer immediately. Her fingers hovered over the door lock. Every nerve in her body screamed caution.

Lord, why tonight?

Her daddy's voice rang in her head: *"If trouble comes knockin', keep one hand on your way out and the other on somethin' solid."*

She weighed her options fast. Leaving her purse in the car meant she wouldn't get robbed, but walking with a stranger in the dead of night? Risky.

She squared her shoulders, studying him. He wasn't much bigger than her—she could take him if she had to.

Yeah, okay. If he tries something crazy, he gon' catch these hands.

She slowly cracked the window. "Where's the nearest phone?"

"There's a gas station under the highway. We gotta take the underpass." He gestured toward the darkened slope leading beneath the overpass. "You'll need to grab my hand."

Pia hesitated.

She had on wedge heels, which meant she'd either twist her ankle or fall on her face if she wasn't careful. The idea of touching a stranger's hand sent another wave of unease crawling up her spine.

But she had no choice.

She sucked in a breath and took his hand, watching him closely as they stepped off the shoulder of the road.

The air beneath the underpass was thick with the sour scent of damp concrete and something muskier—like stale sweat. Each step felt heavier, the darkness pressing in.

"Just hold my hand and walk slow. I promise I won't hurt you," he tried to reassure her.

Pia's mind raced. *If he makes one wrong move—*

Headlights cut through the night.

"Pia!"

Her father's voice.

Pierre's Ford F-250 swerved recklessly into the gas station parking lot, gravel spitting beneath the tires. He jumped out before the truck even fully stopped, his 6'2" frame moving with urgency.

Pia snatched her hand back from the stranger, sprinting toward her father's arms.

"I was so scared," she murmured into his shoulder, trying to hold back tears.

Pierre rubbed her back. "You okay, sweet pea?"

She nodded, still shaken.

Pierre turned to the man. "Hey, man—thank you for helpin' my daughter." He reached into his pocket and pressed a few bills into the man's palm. "I appreciate you."

The man nodded, his expression unreadable, and shuffled back toward the underpass, disappearing into the shadows.

Pierre exhaled sharply. "Let's get outta here."

Pia climbed into the passenger seat of the truck as her father pulled up behind her Honda.

"It'll only take a sec," Pierre said, unbuckling his seatbelt.

"It'll be quicker if I help," Pia offered.

Pierre gave her a look. "No. I just want you to sit tight. Be aware of your surroundings. If you see anything off, you tell me, hear?"

She sighed, rolling down the window. "Yes, sir."

As he pulled the spare tire and tools from the trunk, Pia checked the gas station lights in the distance. The neon glow buzzed faintly.

Then—

A sudden burst of gunfire shattered the stillness.

Two cars tore down the highway, bullets flying between them.

"Dad, get down!" Pia screamed.

Pierre barely had time to react before the hail of bullets ricocheted around them. Pia ducked low onto the floorboard, heart hammering.

Then...something *shifted*.

The air around her pulsed. A green shimmer flickered across her vision for the briefest second.

The bullets—

They didn't hit her father.

Pierre crouched low beside the car, wide-eyed. As the gunfire faded and the cars sped off into the distance, Pia cautiously peeked over the dashboard.

Her father stood up, brushing dust off his jacket.

"I'm okay, sweet pea," he said, almost confused. "And the tire's fixed." He tossed her the keys. "Let's get outta here. I'll follow you home."

Pia's hands trembled as she slid into the driver's seat. She stole a glance at the pavement—bullet casings littered the ground.

But there was no blood. No impact marks where her dad had been standing.

What the hell just happened?

At home, Pia struggled to sleep.

Her alarm blared at 6 a.m., yanking her from restless dreams.

She sat up in bed, blinking against the early morning darkness, the memory of the night before playing on repeat.

The gunfire. The pulsing energy. The way the bullets *missed*.

She shook her head.

I was just seeing things. Right?

Through the wall from across the street, she heard the steady bass of a morning workout playlist.

Abel. Her next door neighborhood.

Rolling her eyes, she threw back the covers and grabbed her phone. First, she checked her messages. Then, her social media.

Her mind still whirled, but she forced herself into routine.

Her father knocked on the door. "Sweet pea, you up?"

"Yeah, Dad," she called back.

Pia's mom was the one who normally made sure she was awake for school until she died in a car wreck. Her dad had been working at the mechanic shop late the evening of the wreck when the police arrived at their home to notify them of the accident. Pia was only 13 years old, and she knew something was wrong as soon as she opened the door. The police waited until her dad arrived to share the news, and it was the first time Pia had ever seen him cry.

"Alright. Got the coffee on. I gotta head in early—promised James I'd finish rebuilding an engine."

Pia smirked. "You don't know how to take a break, do you?"

Pierre chuckled. "Don't know how, don't need to. You need anything before I go?"

"No, I'm good. Don't forget about my dance program tonight at 5."

"Alright, see you tonight."

As he left, Pia stood by the window looking across the street at Abel's house.

She reached for her mother's angel necklace, fingers brushing the familiar metal.

The memory of the green shimmer flashed in her mind again.

Something had happened last night.

And she needed to figure out what.

Pia looked toward his bedroom, she saw that he was staring right back. She held up both hands, signaling that she would be ready in 10 minutes, and he understood.

The crumpled shirt she'd grabbed fell loosely over her 5'6" slim frame and her jeans had collected more holes, revealing her caramel taut legs than its manufacturer had intended. She took one quick look in the mirror, noticing her coils were still tucked in a bun and when she decided that she didn't look 100% terrible, she headed for the coffeepot to fill her thermal on the way out the door.

"You'll never get a date looking like that." Abel grinned as Pia locked the door on her way out.

"Do you suggest I self-indulge in my looks and workout every morning just to admire myself in every reflection I pass?"

"It wouldn't hurt."

"Shut up, Abel, and get in."

Abel climbed into Pia's car, stuffing his long legs inside. The honda was 12 years old, but she kept the maintenance up, so it looked like it was a new car. She took pride in the car that she helped purchase while Abel's 2025 Mustang looked like it collided with a dump truck.

The two attended the community college in their hometown of Windsorville. It was a small, not-so-rural, not-so-city, country town in southwestern Mississippi near the Mississippi River. It was one of those places where everyone knew everyone. What used to be a quiet and quaint town was now plagued with crime, which was happening everywhere.

"Is your phone working?" Abel asked, as he looked at his signal bars.

"Yeah, mine is working fine."

"Call my phone."

"It's going straight to voicemail," Pia said after a few seconds passed. "I called twice."

"I need to see what's wrong with my phone. I just paid my bill," Abel said frustratingly.

"That's what you get for being with Bell Singular," Pia teased.

"Oh, don't act like your phone doesn't stop working once a month," Abel rebutted.

""Touché," Pia replied.

"I need to see your phone," Abel said.

"Who are you trying to call?" Pia asked with a side eye.

"None of your business," Abel laughed.

"Who's the flavor of the week?" Pia inquired.

"You make it sound bad, but if you must know, I'm dating this girl named Meghan," Abel admitted with a sly grin...

"Meghan, that took geometry with us in high school? Really, Abel. That girl is so sweet. Why would you do that?" Pia asked.

"Do what? We're just dating?!" Abel said, annoyed.

"Boy, you don't date. You hunt...and that girl is prey and she don't even know it," Pia said, shaking her head.

"Dang, P, am I that bad?" Abel asked with a chuckle.

"Stop acting like you care. Do her a favor and leave her alone. Get with someone who is more your speed, like...Lilliana," Pia said.

"Been there, done that, and I will neevvvverrr go back!"

"Wait until I tell Zaya about this one," Pia grinned.

"So I can't use your phone to call Meghan?"

CHAPTER TWO

"And five, six, seven, eight, kick, ball, change, down and turn, boom, boom, pop, bring it together now!"

Pia moved through the last steps of her Saturday class, sweat trickling down her temple. The music pulsed through the dance studio; the bass vibrating through the floors. She caught her reflection in the mirror—muscles taut, movements sharp, body completely in sync with the rhythm.

"A'ight, ladies! That's it for today! Y'all were on fire!" Pia clapped her hands, signaling the end of practice. Her students groaned, some reaching for their water bottles, others collapsing onto the wooden floor in exhaustion.

"Miss Pia, we was just getting started!" one of the younger girls whined.

She smirked. "Oh, so y'all wanna go another hour?"

"Nah, we good," the group replied in unison, already grabbing their bags.

Pia laughed. "That's what I thought."

"Miss Dance Captain herself," Zaya grinned, shaking her head. "One day, you're gonna be running your own studio with your name on the wall."

"That's the goal," Pia said, her grin widening. "But for now, I gotta make sure these girls don't embarrass me at the showcase next month."

Zaya looked her up and down. "Mmm-hmm, and you need to make sure you don't embarrass yourself with that wrinkled tank top and them dusty jeans. Girl, where is your sense of fashion?"

Zaya stood 5'7" and 165 pounds. She looked like a celebrity on any given day.

Pia scoffed, grabbing her gym bag. "Look, I ain't got time to be cute all the time like you. What you dressed up for, anyway?"

Zaya did a slow spin, showing off her olive-green ripped jeans, a peanut butter-colored satin blouse, and matching pumps. Zaya's teeth were brilliantly white and you couldn't help but notice against her beautiful dark brown skin. Her gold bangles jingled as she flipped her long, dark curls over her shoulder. "'Cause I was raised right, unlike some people," she teased.

Pia rolled her eyes. "Uh-huh. Where we headed?"

"Liliana's meeting us at the movies. But before that, we eating."

"You already know I'm down for Collin's Kitchen," Pia said, grabbing her hoodie.

"Exactly," Zaya said. "Let's go before the line gets long."

Pia climbed in Zaya's 2020 Black Sport S Jeep Wrangler. Zaya saved up two years to be able to help her parents get her the car of her dreams. Ever since she was a little girl, she wanted a jeep, and it fit her perfectly, Pia thought: stylish yet rugged, just like Zaya. And she drives it like a bat out of hell.

The two pulled up at Collin's Kitchen robotically executing their routine. The scent of fried catfish, candied yams, and greens wrapped around Pia like a warm hug as she stepped inside Collin's Kitchen.

Behind the counter, Miss Cora, the owner, stood with her apron dusted in flour, taking orders like she ran the world. Her salt-and-pepper curls were wrapped up in a scarf, and her gold hoop earrings caught the light as she took another customer's payment.

"Miss Cora," Zaya grinned, sidling up to the counter. "You already know the deal."

Miss Cora side-eyed her. "Lemme guess. Two orders of fried cat-fish, hard, with mac 'n' cheese, yams, and collards? One tea, one lemonade?"

"You know us too well," Pia said.

"'Cause y'all don't switch it up," Miss Cora muttered, shaking her head. "Y'all gon' eat me outta business with all this fish."

Zaya smirked. "Ain't our fault you got the best in town."

Miss Cora chuckled as she rang them up. "Go sit down. I'll bring it out when it's ready."

As Pia and Zaya slid into a booth, Pia felt her phone vibrate. Abel's name popped up.

> **Abel: Movie was good?**

> **Pia: Haven't seen it yet. You should come.**

> **Abel: Have a date.**

Pia rolled her eyes. "Guess who's out here ruining another girl's life?"

Zaya barely looked up from her drink. "Abel?"

"Abel."

"Tell him to get his life together."

"Been saying that for years," Pia muttered, tossing her phone on the table.

"Well, have you met Lilliana's new boo?" Zaya asked.

"No, I haven't," Pia stated.

"For you two to still be in the same town, y'all don't hang much, huh?"

"Lilliana is doing her own thing, working a full-time job. Our schedules always seem to clash. We still talk, or more so, text," Pia said.

"Well, I haven't talked to her yet, but I'm going to ask her about this new guy after the movie. He's Daniel's cousin. Moved here from Louisiana," Zaya said.

"Daniel, who had the shootout on the north side?" Pia asked.

"Yep," Zaya affirmed. "She's even posted him on her Connexta page."

"His whole family is bad business. You know his mom is locked up for killing his dad. What's wrong with Lilliana?" Pia asked in disbelief.

"Chile, I don't know, but we're going to find out today!" Zaya said, amused.

The waitress brought over their dishes, and the two began to feast.

"I hope I can stay awake through the movie," Pia said as she stuffed her face with collard greens.

"Baby, we both gon' have the itis," Zaya laughed.

"We'll, I'm not going to stuff myself too bad," Pia said. She had divided her food in half, part to eat there and the remaining to take home.

"Watch me work," Zaya said and continued to eat every last drop of food.

Zaya drove into an empty parking lot on two wheels in front of the AMC theater.

"Nobody's racing you for this spot. Calm down," Pia said.

"There's Lil. You see. Standing by the door. But I don't see where she parked," Zaya said, ignoring Pia's comment about her driving.

Liliana was petite like Pia, with a light brown complexion and three inches taller. She never went out without makeup, her hair in big loose curls down her back, and stiletto nails and pedicured toes. She wore a black Gucci jumpsuit with lace-up booties to match.

"Hey, boo!" Zaya said, hugging Liliana. "You look niiiccceee!"

"Hey, guys!" Liliana exclaimed.

"Hey, Lil," Pia said, giving the next hug. "Where's your car?"

"Oh, I let Blaze drop me off," Liliana said, blushing. "He needed to run some errands, and he's having car problems. I told him y'all would drop me off at home."

Pia and Zaya exchanged a quick look at one another, then back at Liliana.

"Who's Blaze?" Zaya said with a smile.

"We'll talk. Let's just go and watch this zombie movie. I can't believe I let y'all talk me into this," Liliana groaned.

"Okay, let's, but you're not off the hook," Zaya remarked.

Liliana giggled as the trio entered the theaters.

After two hours, the girls left the theater. The movie was mid, but the food was hitting, so the night still counted as a win.

Zaya drove them back toward the south side of town, Liliana in the backseat fixing her lip gloss.

The radio played, but the streets were quiet. Too quiet.[1]

---

1. **Book Soundtrack Cue**: "Is You Krazy" – Lady London.

As they approached the old bridge over the river, the traffic slowed to a complete stop.

"What's going on?" Pia frowned.

Zaya rolled down her window. "Hey! What's going on up there?" she called to a man standing outside his truck.

"Car accident," he said. "Ain't nobody moving 'til the cops clear it."

Pia exhaled. "Damn. Guess we wait."

The bridge was full of cars waiting to get to their next destination on a Saturday night. Some people had cut their cars off, and others were hanging out on the shoulder walking to and fro.

Liliana sighed dramatically. "If y'all had let me pick the movie, we would've been home by now."

Zaya snorted. "Girl, hush."

"Well, since we may be here a minute," Zaya began, "tell us about this Blaze. How'd you meet?"

"He came into the Bistro about two weeks ago while I was working and asked for my number. I thought he was cute, so I gave it to him," Lil said nonchalantly.

"Two weeks and he's already driving your Lexus?" Zaya asked, astonished.

Then—

A gunshot cracked through the air.

Then another.

Then—chaos.

A black SUV came screeching onto the bridge, gunfire erupting from the windows.

People screamed.

Cars swerved.

Brrrrrt, Brrrrrt, Brrrrrt...

Bullets ripped through windshields, tires, and metal.

"Shit, get down!" Pia yelled..

"What the hell?" Zaya screamed.

Zaya froze, her hands clenched tight on the steering wheel.

"ZAYA, TURN!" Pia screamed, reaching for the wheel.

Zaya snapped out of it, jerking the Jeep left—just in time to dodge a rain of bullets.

The SUV sped past, spraying lead into anything in its path. Forward and backward.

There wasn't anywhere to go on the bridge.

Glass shattered. Metal crunched. A woman's shriek cut through the night.

Liliana screamed from the backseat, curling into a ball.

Pia's pulse slammed in her ears.

Then—

A green glow flickered across the bridge.

For a split second, Pia saw it.

A shield.

Translucent. Shimmering.

The bullets hitting Zaya's Jeep...weren't penetrating.

They bounced.

Rolled off the hood like pebbles on a pond.

That wasn't normal.

Pia's hands trembled. She felt something inside her shift, like a door cracking open.

Then, just as fast as it came—the glow vanished.

The SUV peeled off, tires screeching. The gunfire stopped.

Pia's chest heaved. "Lord, have mercy," Pia said.

Zaya pulled the Jeep to the shoulder, hands shaking on the wheel.

Pia swallowed hard, looking down at her own trembling fingers.

"What... the hell just happened?"

"See, I don't miss this shit one bit," Zaya said. "This is ridiculous!"

Police officers with armed rifles began running past the cars toward the SUV, where the shooting erupted. Other officers were making sure that everyone was in their car because several tried to exit their vehicles once the shooting stopped.

"See, I don't miss this shit one bit," Zaya said. "This is ridiculous."

Traffic began to move, and as the girls crept closer to their exit, they saw cars riddled with bullets. A body was covered with a white blood-stained sheet lying over on the shoulder. There was blood visible on the sheet and the ground. Liliana slowly sat up on the back seat and put her seat belt on.

"Y'all didn't see that?!" Pia questioned.

CHAPTER THREE

L ast night felt like a dream. Pia decided to keep the events to herself, so she didn't upset her dad.

Besides, today was the anniversary of her mom's death, and Pia didn't want anything to shift the focus from celebrating her mom. She and her dad would visit her mom's grave every two Sundays, and today was the day for the much-anticipated visit.

"The flowers held up a long time, didn't they?" Pia said, removing the dead bouquet of roses and replacing them with fresh ones in the granite vase on her mom's tombstone.

"Yes, they did," Pierre responded. He began sweeping dead leaves from the grave.

The gravesite was relatively empty except for Ms. Marie, the shop-keeper, and her son, Tay, who had special needs because of his vision impairment and cognitive delay.

"Dad, I was wondering," Pia began. "I want to know more about my family. Our family is small, so I was thinking about going on Ancestry.com to see if we have any relatives we don't know about."

"You don't need the internet to learn about your family, Pia. I want to show you something when we get home," he said.

As the two began to head back to Pierre's truck, they found themselves walking adjacent to Ms. Marie and Tay.

"Good evening, Mademoiselle and monsieur," Pierre said.

"Good evening," Ms. Marie smiled, showing her dimples. Tay simply smiled and kept moving forward. "Pia, I've been meaning to tell you I've restocked fresh strawberries. You better come by and get some before we sell out."

"Thanks, Ms. Marie. I'll be by this week as soon as I can."

"Okay, I'll try to put you some to the side, sweetie. I know how much you love strawberries. Your mom used to love them, too," Ms. Marie said with a warm smile.

Ms. Marie walked Tay over to a 1969 Buick Skylark. The two climbed inside, and Ms. Marie waved as she pulled off.

"Man, I love that car," Pierre said as he opened his truck door. "Sweet pea, don't you want to get your dad one of those nice antique cars?"

Pia laughed and rolled her eyes.

Back home, Pierre pulled a dusty old box from the hall closet and set it on the coffee table.

Pia eyed it warily. "What's this?"

"Family history," he said simply, lifting the lid.[1]

Inside were old black-and-white photographs, some yellowed with age.

Pia slid next to her dad on the couch and took the lid off the box.

"Now, this first album is one your mom had growing up. This is your mom when she was a baby, and look at this one. This one was when your mom was about 8 years old. I had just moved to Mississippi and your mom was one of the first friends I made here," Pierre explained.

"Aww, that's sweet dad," Pia said. "Look, there's Papa Henry. I miss him," Pia remarked.

"Me too, sweet pea."

---

1. **Book Soundtrack Cue:** .

After a brief pause, Pierre continued, "Here is one of you and your mom," Pierre said.

"I've never seen this one before," Pia said.

Pierre continued to flip through them, pausing on one. He handed it to Pia.

It was a faded portrait of a young woman, dark-skinned with striking features. She looked just like Pia.

Pia's breath caught.

"Who is she?"

Pierre exhaled. "Your great-great-grandmother. Ethel Perlie Webster."

A shiver ran down Pia's spine.

She knew that name.

"Wait. Wasn't she the one that..?"

Pierre nodded. "Vanished. Back in 1959. Folks say she disappeared with her husband and their newborn baby. No trace. No bodies. Nothin'."

Pia swallowed.

He flipped to another photo. A baby. A tiny girl with big, bright eyes.

Pia's stomach dropped.

"She had this," Pierre murmured, pointing to the baby's shoulder.

A moon-shaped birthmark.

The same one Pia had.

Her pulse pounded. "Dad... what do you think happened to them?"

Pierre hesitated. "I don't know, Sweet Pea. But I do know this—your great-grandma Mary was found on a relative's doorstep back in 1959 when she was two years old. No sign of her parents. Just...gone."

Pia's skin tingled.

The air felt heavy.

Something wasn't right.

She flipped through more pictures, her fingers trembling.

Then she noticed something.

A faint green spot.

It wasn't just a stain. It was on every single picture that included Ethel Perlie.

Pia's chest tightened.

She rubbed at the mark, but it wouldn't budge.

"Dad..." Her voice came out quieter than she intended. "You see this?"

Pierre squinted. "Huh. Probably just old film. Pictures fade weird sometimes."

But Pia knew.

That wasn't fading. That was something else. Something alive.

She stared at her great-great-grandmother's face, the eerie familiarity sending goosebumps up her arms.

And then—for the briefest second—

The picture flickered.

Like a pulse of green light.

Pia dropped it.

Pierre looked at her, startled. "You alright?"

Pia forced a shaky laugh. "Yeah. Just tired. Let's look at your side of the family now."

"So, you want to see us Cajuns, huh?" Pierre chuckled.

"Yeah, let's see how many Louisianians there are."

"Despite me having come from a big family, we don't see my family much because we're spread all over the country. A lot of us migrated east, others north and west, and only a few still live in New Orleans," Dad said, pulling out another photo album.

"I wish I could've met your parents," Pia said quietly.

Me too, sweet pea. Here they are, your grandma Lynda and your grandpa Frank Pierce.

"She's pretty," Pia said.

"Yes, she is. Here she is as a baby. Looks kind of like your baby picture, doesn't it?" Pierre commented.

"Yeah, it really does," Pia smiled. "Is that her mom holding her?"

"Yep, your great grandmother Ruth. She died giving birth to my mother."

"And your granddad?"

"That's another tale. People say he couldn't handle losing grandma Ruth. They say he went a bit crazy. Even dabbled in some voodoo to try to bring her back. A lot of family members left around that time. They said things were bad, then, sinister even, and no one wanted to be around."

"So, what happened to him?"

"He was found dead in a marsh. No one is clear how it happened and the coroner had no clear cause of death. That's one of many Pierce family mysteries."

"Ohh...kay, I think I've had enough family history for a while. I better get ready for class in the morning."

"Yeah, I think I'm about to get ready for bed."

"Well, make sure you find something warm to wear tomorrow. We have a cold front coming and the temperature is already dropping outside."

"Yes, ma'am," dad chuckled.

Pia checked the doors, cut off the lights, and was headed to her room when she decided to double back to the box on the table. She swiped the portrait of Ethel Perlie from the stack and slipped it into her pocket. Then she slid the picture of her and her mom out of the photo album and disappeared into her room.

CHAPTER FOUR

"**D**ue to inclement weather, Northwest Community College will be closed Wednesday, February 12, 2025," Pia read aloud from her phone. A slow grin spread across her face. "Yesss, I get to sleep in."

She was stretched out on the couch, scrolling through her school's Connexta page, while her father, Pierre, sat nearby unlacing his boots after a long day's work.

"I hope that weatherman ain't lying again," Pierre muttered. "School always shutting down, and half the time ain't even a drop of rain."

Pia smirked. "That's 'cause God knows we need a break, even if y'all stubborn workaholics don't."

Pierre chuckled. "Well, I know one thing—I'll still be at work in the morning."

"My point exactly," Pia said, shaking her head. "You don't know when to sit down somewhere."

Pierre grinned, stretching his legs out. "Don't you got somewhere to be?"

"Yeah, dance class in an hour. I wish the storm would just go ahead and start so I could stay home." Pia groaned, stretching.

"It'll be over before you know it, Sweet Pea," Pierre reassured her.

Pia sighed, knowing he was right. "I guess I better get going."

Pierre stood up. "When you get back, I'll have dinner ready."

Pia eyed him suspiciously. "Please don't tell me it's breakfast for dinner again."

Pierre laughed. "Oh, you got jokes? That ain't the only thing I know how to cook. I was thinking...pizza."

"Now that sounds about right," Pia said. "Just make sure you get Alfredo with chicken, spinach, and tomatoes—thin crust—with ranch and buffalo sauce."

Pierre shook his head, amused. "I know, I know, I know. And a pepperoni for me."

"Good," Pia said, giving him a quick hug. "See you later, Dad."

She grabbed her bag and headed out the door.

Pia pulled into the studio parking lot and immediately knew something was off.

A man stood in front of the studio door.[1]

It wasn't that a few girls were already waiting outside—some of them liked showing up early—but men never came to the studio door. Fathers, uncles, and brothers always stayed in their cars, honking when needed.

This was different.

Pia parked and got out, her senses on high alert.

"Can I help you?" she asked, keeping her voice even but firm.

The man turned, offering a polite smile. "Hi, I'm Raymond Windham. I'm the new president over at the Masonic lodge across the street." He gestured toward the brick building with the old Masonic emblem. "I've been visiting all the businesses on this strip, checking in before the storm. It's supposed to be bad, so I just wanted to see if y'all needed any help preparing."

---

1. **Book Soundtrack Cue**: "The Hills" – The Weeknd.

Pia studied him. He was tall—maybe 6'2"—with brownish-red hair, blue eyes, and a dimple on his right cheek. His face was youthful, but something about him felt...older. He wore gray slacks and a white button-up, topped with a black-brimmed hat.

And he chewed his gum like it was the last meal on Earth.

Pia nodded slowly. "I think we're good. After tonight, we're closing until the freeze is over, so no one will be using this building."

Raymond rocked back on his heels. "Gotcha. Well, if anything comes up, just give one of us a holler. We'll be right there, happy to help."

"Thanks," Pia said. "I'll keep that in mind."

Raymond tipped his hat before walking off down the sidewalk.

From across the parking lot, Ms. Mabel watched the entire exchange.

She sat in her 1984 Buick LeSabre. The driver's side window rolled down just enough for her voice to carry.

"You seen him before?" she asked.

Pia shook her head. "No, ma'am."

Ms. Mabel clicked her tongue, eyes narrowing as she followed Raymond's retreating figure. "Mmmhmm. Well, I'll be sitting right here 'til practice is over. Ain't no sense in running my errands when there's strangers pokin' around.'"

Pia smiled. "Yes, ma'am. Thank you."

She unlocked the studio door and let the girls inside, but the uneasy feeling in her stomach lingered.

Despite her initial hesitation about coming, practice was electric.

The girls learned five new eight-counts, and they added freestyle solos for their upcoming spring performance. Pia was impressed—some of the girls tapped into a confidence she hadn't seen before.

They ran thirty minutes over, lost in the music, in the rhythm, in the joy of movement.

If Ms. Mabel hadn't gotten out of her car to knock on the door, they probably would've kept going.

"Alright, ladies," Pia called. "Once this storm blows over, I'll let y'all know when the next practice will be. The freeze is supposed to last three days, but we'll see. Stay safe, and I'll be in touch!"

The girls grabbed their belongings and hurried out.

Pia stayed behind to lock up, but something nagged at her.

On instinct, she checked her phone.

Her weather app wouldn't refresh.

Her social media? Not loading.

She frowned, shutting her phone off and back on. Still nothing.

Pia dialed her dad.

Nothing.

Not even a ring.

What the hell?

Knock, knock, knock!

Pia jumped, her heart slamming against her ribs.

She turned to see Raymond standing at her driver's side window.

She hesitated, then rolled it down slightly.

"My bad," Raymond said, hands up. "Didn't mean to scare you, Ms...."

"Pia," she said, her voice tighter than before.

"Ms. Pia," he repeated, nodding. "Saw you sitting here. Everything alright?"

Pia forced a small smile. "Yeah, I was just leaving."

Raymond nodded. "Well, have a good night, ma'am."

Pia didn't answer.

She just drove off, the hairs on her arms standing on end. She couldn't wait to get home to her dad.

As soon as Pia stepped inside, the smell of warm pizza wrapped around her.

"It's in the oven, Sweet Pea," Pierre called. "Kept it warm for you."

"Thanks, Dad," Pia sighed, realizing how hungry she actually was.

Pierre glanced at her as she grabbed a plate. "How was practice?"

"It was good. But some guy from the Masonic lodge came by, asking if we needed help with the storm."

Pierre's face darkened. "What man?"

"He said his name was Raymond something."

Pierre set his drink down. "The lodge across from the studio?"

"Yeah, that's what he said."

Pierre's jaw tightened. "I'll have to pay them a visit. See who's checking up on my baby. You can never be too safe, Pia. Always be aware of your surroundings. Don't trust anyone."

"I know, Daddy," Pia said. "I told him we didn't need anything."

"Good." Pierre exhaled. "And if these roads ice over, looks like I'll be stuck in here with you tomorrow."

Pia smirked. "Yay! Movie marathon all day."

Pierre chuckled. "Sounds like a plan, Sweet Pea."

But Pia's mind was elsewhere.

Because something told her...

Raymond Windham wasn't just checking in.

And for the first time in a long time—

Pia didn't feel safe.

She also couldn't shake the picture of Ethel Perlie Webster.

The woman in the picture looked too much like her for it to be a coincidence. Same high cheekbones. Same deep brown skin. Same eyes that seemed to hold something unspoken.

And that green mark...

It wasn't a stain.

It had been something else.

Something alive.

"You sure you alright, Sweet Pea?"

Pierre's voice yanked her back to the present. He stood near the sink, arms crossed, studying her with the kind of look that saw straight through her.

She set the picture down and forced a smile. "Yeah, just thinking."

Pierre grunted, unconvinced.

"Mmm-hmm," he muttered, taking a sip of his drink. "Thinkin' is good. Thinkin' too much and not actin'... that's when you get stuck."

Pia exhaled, rubbing her temples. "Daddy, can I ask you something?"

Pierre set his cup down. "Course, baby. What's on your mind?"

She hesitated. "Did Grandma Mary ever... say anything about her mother? About Ethel?"

Pierre's lips pressed into a thin line. "Not much," he admitted after a pause. "She never liked to talk about that part of the family. Always said some things was better left in the past."

Pia frowned. "But why?"

Pierre let out a slow breath. "Your grandma... she had a way of knowing things before they happened. She'd dream about things, feel things most folks couldn't. Said it came from her mother's side."

Pia's stomach tightened.

That sounded too familiar.

Pierre leaned in slightly. "Why you askin'?"

Pia opened her mouth. Then closed it.

If she told him about the bullets on the bridge—how they should've hit them but somehow didn't—would he believe her?

She wasn't sure she even believed it herself.

Instead, she just shook her head. "No reason. Let's watch tv."

Pierre didn't push. He just gave her that same knowing look, the one that said he could read between the lines even if she didn't say the words.

"I heard the Kindred series on Hulu is good," Pia told her dad as she searched for something for them to watch.

"Sounds good to me," Pierre said, sitting down in his recliner under an old quilt.

Ding-dong

"The temperature has really dropped outside. I wonder who that is," Pia asked as she headed to the door. "Oh, it's just Abel."

Pia opened the door and headed back to her seat on the couch. Abel was bundled up in a parka and matching Sorel's.

"Hello to you, too," Abel said to Pia. "Hello, Mr. Pierce."

"Hey, Abel. You came to join the party," Pierre chuckled.

"Yeah, it's too quiet at my house."

"I thought you would've been keeping Meghan warm," Pia teased.

"No, we broke up. I'm seeing Brooklyn now," Abel grinned. "But she's out of town."

Pia's mouth dropped as she shook her head in disbelief.

"Well, you're just in time. We're about to watch TV," Pierre said.

"Cool. Pia...I tried to call you earlier. Is your phone working?"

"I don't know what was wrong with it," Pia said.

"First my phone, then your phone. I'm starting to think there may be some truth to what people are saying on Connexta."

"Abel, I don't entertain conspiracy theories," Pia sighed.

"Well, when the country erupts in civil war, don't say I didn't warn you," Abel said, unzipping his jacket.

"What are people saying?" Pierre asked, intrigued.

"Some people are saying that the government causes these phone glitches. They're saying that it's some kind of government testing," Abel explained.

"For what reason?"

"For the same reason as all historical groups of power–to take over the world," Abel said confidently.

"Dad, don't pay him any mind. Abel loves to talk conspiracies and the groups he joins online don't make it any better," Pia said with an eye roll.

"Hey, I'm just the messenger. Believe what you want."

"We will," Pia responded. "Now, let's see if this series measures up to the book."

"It rarely does, sweet pea."

CHAPTER FIVE

T he mechanic shop was packed with cars battered by the two-day storm. If it wasn't a wreck, it was dead batteries or ice in the fuel lines. Pierre was swamped, but he thrived in the hum of a well-tuned engine. While he worked, you could hear the tunes of Al Green's "Let's Stay Together" pouring through the bluetooth speaker.

"Hey, stranger," a sultry voice called as Pierre worked under a 2013 Kia Sorento.

Sliding from beneath the car, he grinned. Rosa Jimenez stood before him in a winter white cashmere pantsuit, six-inch Bottega boots clicking against the concrete. Her honeyed skin glowed, and her sleek, blowout curls cascaded over her shoulders. Pierre wiped his hands on a cloth hanging from his pocket.

"You know you can call me Rosa," she purred, rolling the 'R' like a melody.

"Yes, Rosa. How can I be of service?"

"The dealership is backed up, and I need to see what's wrong with my baby."

"The BMW?"

"No, the Caddy."

"What's going on with it?"

"It won't go into boost. It has to be the weather, right? Un problema tras otro!"

"I'll take a look on my break," Pierre compromised.

"Oh, thank you, Papi!" Rosa cooed, handing over her keys.

"Tell Lilliana I said hello."

"I sure will." *She turned, hips swaying, leaving the scent of jasmine and spice in her wake.*

"Oh my gosh, Lilliana, it smells like straight-up *loud* in here! Let this window down."[1]

"Mom, what? I don't smell anything," Lilliana scoffed.

Rosa wrinkled her nose. "Have you been smoking weed?!"

"No! That had to be from Blaze."

"Is that why his name is Blaze?" Rosa asked, side-eyeing her daughter. "And why are you dating a *dope boy*?"

"Mom, it's not like that. And I *like* him."

"Well, he better treat you right or I'll have your cousin Carlyta put a root on him."

Lilliana's ears perked. "What's a root?"

Rosa smirked. "It's Brujeria. Spells, protection, curses... depends on the intention."

"Wait, you're serious?"

Rosa tapped her nails against the wheel. "Serious enough. You ever wonder how your Uncle Raynard kept hitting the lottery? That was *Lita*—Carlyta Boudreaux, down in New Orleans. She's been deep in the craft since we were kids. Folks used to come from all

---

1. **Book Soundtrack Cue**: "Mask off" – Future.

over the parish to get work done by Aunt Estelle, and Lita inherited her gift."

"Could she really put a spell on someone?"

"Some folks swear by it." Rosa gave her a knowing look. "Why? You worried about your man?"

Lilliana bit her lip. "Nah. Just curious."

"Baby, you don't need magic when you got money. That's power enough," Rosa stated. Now, let's get to the spa before we miss our appointment.

"Ok, but I'm meeting up with Blaze for lunch," Lil said.

"Well, I guess you should take me home after the spa, and I'll call you when my truck is ready," Rosa said.

Lilliana pulled into Blaze's neighborhood—a row of shotgun houses, each porch occupied by men in hoodies, twisting up cigars and eyeing her car like a foreigner had stepped onto sacred ground.

It was a hard contrast to her home that stood tall on 4,200 square feet and included five bedrooms, four bathrooms, an outdoor kitchen, a library, a home office, a home gym, an in-ground pool, an in-law suite, and a three-car garage.

She exhaled, gripping the steering wheel. She watched as Daniel was standing on the porch, adding bullets to his extended clip. Blaze emerged from the house, head nodding to his people as he hopped in.

"Hey, bae," Lilliana said. She rubbed his back, outlining his skull in fire tattoo with the tips of her finger, and kissed him on his cheek.

"I'm driving," he said, sparking a blunt.

"Where we going?"

"Don't worry about it. Just ride."

Lilliana pursed her lips. "My mom already said she'll have my cousin do her *Voodoo* on you."

Blaze chuckled, blowing smoke out the window. "Tell Moms to chill. You know I'm good to you."

"You better be," Lil said flirtatiously.

Lilliana thought about what her mom said as she dropped her off after the spa date: "And make sure Blaze is on his best behavior or I have two words: Cousin Dominique."

"I thought we didn't need spells," Lil said as she rolled up the window and began backing out of the driveway.

Lilliana enjoyed her mother's protectiveness.

The 'quick errand' turned into two hours of Blaze chopping it up with some dude about guns and money. Lilliana's stomach growled. When he finally slid back in, she was *heated*.

"So what you wanna eat?"

"Anything. I'm starving."

"You been eating a lot lately," he teased. "Better keep that body right."

Lilliana forced a smile, but her jaw clenched.

They pulled up at Collins, ready to dig into the catfish po'boys and fried okra. As they stepped inside, Lilliana's stomach twisted. *Pia was here—with Abel. Their eyes locked, and before she could escape, Pia was already at their table.*

"Oh, lord, here she comes," Lil said under her breath.

Blaze looked up and smiled like a Chester cat.

"Hey, Lil!" Pia said.

"Hey, girl! How are you?!" Lilliana plastered on a fake grin.

"I'm good," Pia responded.

"Hey, Abel!" Lilliana said.

"What's up, Lilliana?"

"Pia, Abel, I want y'all to meet my boyfriend, Blaze."

The guys shook hands while Pia waved.

"Girl, we are stuffed. We're about to leave, but it was good seeing you. We need to catch up," Pia said.

"Yes, girl, I was thinking the same thing. Let's do lunch next week," Lil said excitedly.

"Okay, sounds like a plan. See you then. And nice to meet you, Blaze," Pia said as she and Abel headed for the door.

"Fa'sho," Blaze responded.

The waitress came with the food and sat it on the table.

Blaze eyed Pia up and down. "Damn, she fine. She an athlete?"

Lilliana's blood ran hot. "She's a dancer."

Blaze smirked. "Figures. She look *good*."

Lilliana stabbed at her food, appetite gone. *Maybe cousin Carlyta could work something on Miss Perfect... just a little something to make her disappear.*

"This looks good! I'm ready to eat," Blaze said.

Lilliana sat there fuming, her face turning more and more crimson with every second. She had barely touched her plate when a text came through that read: *My truck is ready.*

CHAPTER SIX

"Pia, I'm headed to work. I'll see you later," Pierre called as he grabbed his keys from the counter.

"Okay, Dad. Have a good day," Pia responded, barely looking up from her phone.

She was staring at a friend request from someone named Perlie Boudreaux. The account was new—too new. No mutual friends. But the profile picture stopped her cold. The woman looked eerily like her mother, and they shared the same last name. Pia's stomach tightened. *Who was this?* She hovered over the "Accept" button but decided to leave it alone for now. *Not today.* She had plans.

Saturday morning sunlight poured through the blinds, washing the living room in a soft glow. Just two days ago, ice had blanketed the streets, but now, warmth had returned like winter never happened.

Even though the sun was shining brightly, the day had a quiet stillness to it. Outside, birds chattered, and the world moved slow—the way it always did in the South after a storm.

Pia finished the last spoonful of her Cinnamon Toast Crunch and tossed on a pair of jeans, a cropped hoodie, and her favorite gold hoops. There was no dance class today, so she decided today would be good to take a trip to Ms. Marie's shop. It was still early, and Pia loved to shop before the crowd came. She jotted down a quick grocery list and grabbed her keys.

The Mississippi River Market sat at the waterfront, a strip lined with mom-and-pop shops, thrift stores, and food vendors selling everything from fried catfish to pralines. Pia pulled up in front of Ms. Marie's, the only grocery store on the strip. There were few people at the market that early in the morning. The air smelled like sweetgrass and barbecue smoke from a food truck setting up nearby. The Mississippi River stretched serenely behind the strip. She only saw a few old heads already camped out with fishing rods, their coolers propped open beside them. She grabbed two recyclable bags from her trunk and went inside.

As she stepped out of the car, the familiar sound of Whitney Houston crooned softly from a speaker inside the store. A warm breeze carried the scent of Shea butter and incense through the air. She smiled.

"Morning, Ms. Marie," Pia greeted as she walked in.

Ms. Marie, standing behind the counter in a flowy yellow sundress and a green-and-yellow shawl, gave her a knowing smile. "Morning, baby girl. You up early."

"Trying to beat the crowd."

Tay smiled and held the door.

"Good to see you, Pia," Ms. Marie said.

Pia jumped as the door slammed. She should be used to Tay and his habits. He liked to keep doors closed and lights off. For that reason, Ms. Marie's shop was brightened by sunlight and the only electric light was in the freezer and on the touch screen register on the counter at checkout. Nobody minded Tay's ways. He was as sweet as bear meat and as gentle as a lamb.

"Thank you, Tay," Pia responded with a giggle.

Tay sat back down in his rocking chair by the door. He just nodded and rocked on.

Pia moved through the aisles, picking up her and her dad's favorites—red beans, smoked turkey necks, Blue Bell ice cream. She tossed in a bottle of Ms. Marie's homemade hot sauce, labeled with a handwritten tag. Everybody swore by it, and she wasn't about to run out.

At checkout, Ms. Marie didn't wear a lick of makeup, but her skin shone bronze in the sunlight.

"Did you find everything you needed?" Ms. Marie asked.

"Yes, ma'am, I sure did." Pia said. "I even found…"

Her voice cut off. Out of the corner of her eye, she saw it- a green light out of her peripheral. The light seemed to be beaming-no, *pulsing*-right under the water near the river bank.

"You alright, baby?" Ms. Marie asked.

"Yes, ma'am," Pia said quickly. "Can I sit these bags here for just a second? I'll be right back."

"Go on," Ms. Marie responded, giving a slight nod.

Pia walked out to the river to get a closer look. The light was still there, beaming brilliantly underneath the surface of the water. It felt like she was being drawn to it.

Pia bent down and grazed the water with her fingers. It felt smooth and cool against her skin. As she continued, ripples began to dance across the water. The river felt tranquil…maybe even familiar, like an old song she couldn't remember the words to.

As she leaned toward the light that beamed beneath, the river hugged her in a tight grip, pulling her into its depth.

Panic flared in her chest. She kicked, flailed, but the current held her tight, wrapping around her like unseen hands. She tried to swim, but it seemed like she was going nowhere. Her movements were frantic and desperate. She flailed her arms, yet she could see no one coming to her rescue. The water was chaotic, like a storm with no direction.

Her limbs grew tired. She sank, the world going quiet except for the thundering beat of her own heart. The river roared around her, churning like a storm with no wind. She was losing. Drowning.

Just before the darkness closed in, something shimmered beneath her—the outline of something massive, ancient, *alive*. Scales, iridescent and silver-blue, flashed for only a second. A pair of golden eyes locked with hers through the current.

A dragon.

No. That couldn't be right. She blinked, bubbles escaping her lips. It had to be her mind playing tricks. A hallucination brought on by panic and lack of air.

But the eyes—those eyes—stayed with her even as the shadows pulled her deeper.

When she came back up, it seemed that Ms. Marie and her shop were specks away. She tried not to panic, but Pia was scared, really scared. She began swimming again, but was fighting a losing battle. It was as if the Pia and the river were struggling to get in sync. Pia realized she may not see her dad again.

Then something shifted.

As she decided to go back under once more, there was a strange sensation in the water. Every droplet of water seemed to move at her command and her body began to float above the water. She felt a strange sensation come over her, an energy she couldn't explain. It was as if something ancient and powerful had awakened in her. When she reached her hands out, it felt like she was in a bubble, but she couldn't see a bubble...only the green glow that emanated from her being. It wasn't coming from the river anymore.

It was coming from *her*.

Pia drifted over the river back to the river bank and landed softly on the grass right by Ms. Marie. The river was still. No glow. Just Ms. Marie standing over her, completely unfazed.

"Are you okay, child? Let's get you dry," Ms. Marie said calmly.[1]

Pia's breath came in short bursts. What the hell just happened?! Pia thought. She looked around, but no one had seen her except Ms. Marie. The fishermen never looked up. *Did Ms. Marie see that? Did she see me float above water?! Did I just FLOAT above water??!!*

Pia followed Ms. Marie inside the shop, where Ms. Marie handed her a towel so she could dry off.

"I have some clothes in the back. I'll get them for you."

---

1. **Book Soundtrack Cue**: "I'll Find You" – Lecrae ft. Tori Kelly.

Pia, dripping wet, created a puddle around her. She wrung the bottom of her shirt and pulled her hair down out of the bun.

"How did you fall in?" Ms. Marie asked, passing Pia the dry clothes.

"Umm, I'm not sure. It all happened so fast," Pia said nervously. "I'm not even sure how I got back on land."

"You brought yourself back, silly girl," Ms. Marie laughed.

"Brought myself back?" Pia repeated unsurely.

"Yes, baby girl, and in good time, too. But I wasn't gon' let nothing happen to you. I just needed to see if you could do it yourself."

"Ms. Marie, what are you talkin' about?" Pia asked, confused.

"Pia, you have a gift…a power. I didn't understand it myself when I was your age, but I learned how to control it, and you will, too."

Pia didn't know if she was dreaming or had a lack of oxygen from being under the water. She couldn't be hearing Ms. Marie right. *Power? That's not real life! Superheroes have powers! Villains have powers! Not college girls in small* towns, *and definitely not one from Mississippi. And did she really see a dragon?*

Ms. Marie smiled. "It's a lot to take in, I know. You don't have to talk about it now. You don't even have to tell nobody. It'll be our little secret."

Pia's head spun. She turned to Tay, who was still rocking, still smiling like he already knew.

"Tay, bring me the mop so I can get this water off the floor. The last thing I need is for someone to come in here and slip."

Tay handed Ms. Marie the mop, and as she knelt down, her shawl revealed a moon-shaped birthmark on her shoulder. Ms. Marie looked up and saw Pia staring at her shoulder, and she shifted her shawl back into place and continued mopping.

"I have that same birthmark," Pia whispered..

Ms. Marie just smiled. "I know."

CHAPTER SEVEN

"Where are we?" Pia asked Ms. Marie as they rode up a winding hill toward a house that looked like it belonged in another century.

"I want to show you something," Ms. Marie said.

Pia leaned forward in her seat as the car slowed in front of a towering Victorian home, its wrap-around porch lined with wicker chairs and potted ferns. The house was massive—three or four stories at least—with ivy creeping up its brick walls. Thick oak trees, draped in Spanish moss, stood like sentinels around the property. Beyond them, the river stretched so close to the house Pia swore you could touch the water from the back steps.

"Do you live here?"

"Sometimes," Ms. Marie smirked.

Tay stepped out first and settled in the rocking chair that sat near the front door. He moved slow, deliberate—like time never rushed him. Ms. Marie motioned for Pia to follow as she stepped inside.

"Welcome to Windsor Mansion. Are you coming?" Ms. Marie turned and asked Pia, who seemed in awe of the home.

The house smelled of cedarwood, lemon balm, and something ancient. The high ceilings and crown molding spoke of old money, but the house itself felt lived in. Warm. The kind of place where secrets clung to the air like perfume.

Pia's eyes landed on a heavy wooden door near the parlor, covered in iron locks.

"What's in there?" she asked.

Ms. Marie didn't even break stride. "You're not ready for that answer, child."

The parlor was filled with antique furniture, a large fireplace, and floor-to-ceiling bookshelves. One wall had pictures of people Pia assumed to be Ms. Marie's family–generations of black faces, proud and unmoving, their eyes filled with stories Pia couldn't yet understand.

"Pia, what do you think happened today?"

"I'm still trying to figure it out," Pia said uncertainly.

"Is this the first time you've used your gift?" Marie asked.

"I guess so," Pia blinked.

"Think child!" Ms. Marie pressed.

Pia's mind flashed to moments she had never discussed before. The bullet shells near her father that somehow missed him. The time Zaya's Jeep should've been filled with bullet holes. Her stomach clenched.

"There were... moments. Things that should've gone bad, but didn't."

Ms. Marie nodded. "That was you, baby. Your power. You were protecting them, whether you knew it or not."

Pia swallowed hard. "Why is this happening to me?"[1]

Ms. Marie gestured toward the wall of photos. "Look carefully. Do you recognize anyone?"

Pia stepped closer, scanning the rows of faces. Her breath caught in her throat when she saw it—a familiar smile, the same high cheekbones. One picture that caused tears to well up in her eyes.

"Why do you have a picture of my mom?" Pia asked.

---

1. **Book Soundtrack Cue:** "Spirit" – Beyoncé.

Ms. Marie's gaze softened. "You mean, why do I have a picture of my great granddaughter?"

Pia looked up at Ms. Marie like she had seen a ghost. "Great granddaughter?" Pia whispered.

"No need to be scared now. Have a seat," Ms. Marie gestured.

Pia grabbed the arm of a nearby chair and slid into it. She looked towards the door.

"You can't run from this Pia. It's your destiny," Ms. Marie stated.

"But you're supposed to be dead."

"True, but on the day I was born, I used my power, along with my mother's, and together we stopped two shotgun slugs from killing us. When we came out of that hole alive, Mr. Beaumont fell dead right there from a heart attack and his two boys fled like their lives depended on it. For fear of retaliation, we moved down here and laid low. Not even our family knew where we were."

Pia wiped a single tear that escaped down her cheek. "This is too much."

"I'm sure it feels like that now, but there's so much more. I'm not gon' force this on you, Pia. So, I'm going to ask you one time. Do you want to learn about your powers and family history or not?"

Pia sat quietly, contemplating the question. All she wanted was normal. All she wanted was to be home with her dad, hanging out with Abel and Zaya, or dancing at the studio. Now, the town's grocer is telling her she comes from a family of supernaturals?! This can't be real life.

"Well, I'll take that as a no. I'll take you back to your car," Ms. Marie said as she turned toward the door.

"Wait..." Pia stood up and walk toward her mom's picture. "I want to know."

Ms. Marie smiled. "Then let's start from the beginning."

"In the beginning," Ms. Marie started, "before the world was as you know it, there was a war between light and darkness."

"Are you seriously telling me a Bible story?" Pia sighed.

Ms. Marie raised an eyebrow. "Are you a believer?"

Pia nodded. "Yeah. We don't go to church much, but I believe in God."

"Good," Ms. Marie said. "Now hush and listen."

Ms. Marie continued, "After God created man, darkness tried to corrupt the world. Evil spirits walked among the people, feeding on fear, causing chaos. Humanity cried out for protection. And so, the Most High sent down the Nuru'el—the Light of God."

Pia's breath hitched.

"The Nuru'el were celestial beings, meant to guide and protect. But some among them... they fell too deep in love with humanity. They gave their power too freely, created children with human women."

"The Nephilim," Pia whispered.

Ms. Marie nodded. "That's what some call them. But our people? We knew them as the Nurus. The Chosen. Beings who carried divine energy but walked as men."

Pia nodded, showing she understood.

"Our family was one of the first. Each Nuru had a gift—the power of protection, of foresight, of healing, of strength. And those who mastered themselves... those who proved worthy... could ascend beyond their mortal shells."

Pia's mind reeled. "Ascend?"

Ms. Marie leaned forward. "Some call them angels. Others, gods. But we know the truth. The strongest among us don't just awaken their power...they transform."

Pia barely whispered the word. "Into what?"

Ms. Marie smiled. "Dragons."

Silence settled between them.

After a brief pause, Ms. Marie said, "You can speak now."

Pia thought for a moment, her breath shaky. "So... I can heal?"

"And so much more. It makes sense that your power of protection surfaced first. I just have to show you how to tap into your other powers. But Pia...using your powers is a great responsibility. You cannot take this lightly."

Pia nodded. "I want to learn."

"And Pia...many people don't understand our powers. What they don't understand, they fear. What they fear, they attack. You must show no one what you can do."

"Not even my dad?" Pia asked.

"No, child, not even Pierre. So, let us begin. First, you must understand that our power comes from light, which is a source of energy, and there is energy all around us and within us. I want to show you how to heal with light energy."

Ms. Marie began digging through her purse until she found a needle. She pricked her finger and a red dot emerged.

"Ok, now feel the energy. I want you to visualize the purest light and use that light to heal my finger," Ms. Marie instructed.

Pia closed her eyes and focused, drawing on the energy within her. She visualized the light, pure and radiant, flowing through her hands and onto Ms. Marie's finger. Slowly, a soft glow began to emanate from her palms. As the glow intensified, the wound began to close, and the bleeding stopped.

Pia opened her eyes and let out a breath she didn't realize she had been holding. She gently dropped her hands by her side, and she looked up at her with wide eyes.

"You're a natural, Pia."

CHAPTER EIGHT

"Focus, Pia," Ms. Marie's voice was calm, yet commanding, resonating with a power that accented her poised appearance. Her presence was regal, wrapped in an elegance that spoke of Sunday mornings in church and wisdom passed down over pots of gumbo.[1]

"Start with healing. Remember, it's not about forcing the energy, but guiding it," she continued.

For the past week, Pia had been training under Ms. Marie, learning to harness the power she barely understood. They often met at the studio or Ms. Marie's mansion, depending on how much discretion was needed.

Pia stood in the middle of the Windsor mansion, her breath coming in slow, measured puffs. She nodded and closed her eyes to center herself. She stretched out her hands, palms up, and imagined

---

1. **Book Soundtrack Cue**: "Rise Up" – Andra Day.

the flow of life within her. It was a warm, golden river, coursing through her veins. She visualized directing it to her hands, feeling a tingling warmth build up.

"Good," her great-grandmother murmured approvingly. "Now, repeat after me: Praise the Lord, my soul, and forget not all his benefits—who forgives all your sins and heals all your diseases."

Pia opened her eyes just as Ms. Marie made a small incision on her forearm. A bead of crimson welled up, stark against her smooth brown skin. Without hesitation, Pia placed her hands over the wound and closed her eyes again. She whispered the scripture, feeling the warmth radiate from her palms. A soft golden glow seeped into the cut, knitting the skin back together as if it had never been broken.

"Excellent, Pia. You're getting stronger," Ms. Marie said, a hint of pride in her voice.

Pia felt a swell of satisfaction, but quickly tempered it. There was more she had to learn. Rising, she faced her great-grandmother again.

"Now, the energy blast," the Ms. Marie instructed. "This requires control and precision. Gather the energy, but release it with intention."

Pia had been struggling with the energy blasts. Her focus is always off somehow. She took a deep breath, pulling energy from the air around her, from the earth beneath her feet, and from the wellspring within her. She held out her hand, palm facing outward, and concentrated. A sphere of shimmering green light formed, growing brighter and more intense with each passing second. With a swift, deliberate motion, she thrust her hand forward, sending the blast toward a nearby open window.

Instead, the blast veered off course, slamming into the wooden paneling with a crack, splintering it into dust.

"It's okay," her great-grandmother exclaimed. "You'll get it. You've already mastered the force field. The energy blast will require you to maintain a constant flow of energy while holding your focus."

Pia nodded, feeling the weight of her failure.

Sensing Pia's defeat, Ms. Marie said, "Let's do the force field again."

Pia spread her arms wide, feeling the energy form a barrier around her. It was invisible, but she could sense it, like a protective cocoon. She took a step forward, the field moving with her.

Ms. Marie walked up to her, extending a hand. "Hold it steady, Pia."

Pia concentrated, reinforcing the barrier. Her great-grandmother's hand met the force field and stopped, unable to penetrate the invisible shield.

"Perfect," she said with a smile. "Now, release it."

Pia let out a breath she didn't realize she was holding, and the barrier dissipated, the energy returning to the earth and the air around her.

"You've done well today, Pia. But remember, these powers are not just for show. They come with responsibility. You must use them wisely and for the right reasons."

"I understand," Pia replied, her voice steady.

Ms. Marie smiled, a twinkle in her eye. "Tomorrow, we'll work on the energy blast again. But for now, rest. You've earned it."

Pia walked over to the wall she blew up and knelt down to touch the dust. As she stood back up, she caught a black sedan creeping out of the driveway.

"There's a car outside," Pia yelled.

Ms. Marie rushed to the window but only caught a glimpse of taillights disappearing down the street

"Tay!" she yelled as she hurried to the front porch with Pia on her heel.

Tay, rocking on the porch, lifted his chin. His brown skin gleamed under the streetlamp, and without a word, he flicked his wrist, summoning a brief shimmer of energy before letting it vanish. A silent confirmation. He had sensed it, too.

"Could you see anyone in there, child?" Marie inquired as she turned to look at Pia.

"Wait...Tay has powers too?" Pia exclaimed.

"Yes, child, now did you see anyone?"

"No, the windows were tinted," Pia said.

"They went through a lot of trouble not to be seen," Ms. Marie muttered. "No worries. I will find out who that was."

"Do you have cameras?"

"No, I never needed any...and I still don't," Ms. Marie assured Pia.

"I don't see what good having foresight is if we can't see everything," Pia said.

"We see what we need to, but no worries. I *will* find out who that was," Ms. Marie stated.

"You should head on home."

"Should I come back tomorrow?" Pia asked.

"I'll let you know," Ms. Marie said as she pulled Tay up from the rocking chair and led him inside.

As Pia climbed into the car, her phone rang.

"Hey, dad," she said.

"Hey, sweet pea. Where are you?" Pierre asked.

"I'm giving Ms. Marie a dance lesson," Pia lied.

She bit her lip, guilt settling in her chest. How could she tell her father about all this? Would he even believe her?

"Okay, sweet pea," Dad said, his voice tinged with trust.

"I'll see you in a bit," she responded and hung up the phone. Pia tried to suppress the butterflies that fluttered in her stomach as she compounded the anxiety of the unknown car with the guilt of talking to her dad.

Pia pulled into her driveway and parked beside her dad's truck. Before she could step her foot on the ground, Abel was opening the driver's side door.

"Hey, stranger," Abel said, grinning. "You've been ghosting us lately."

"Yeah, I've been busy. What's up?" Pia asked, heading toward the front door.

"Busy doing what?" Abel inquired.

"I've been giving Ms. Marie dance lessons. I'm teaching her ballroom dance," Pia said.

"Yeah, your dad told me that. So I went by your studio. Funny thing, tho. I didn't see you or Ms. Marie," Abel stated.

"Well, sometimes I teach her at her home. There's so much space there and it's more convenient for her."

"Or, hear me out, you could've been taken by the government to spy on us and you're using Ms. Marie as a coverup," Abel explained.

"I can't roll my eyes hard enough. Please stop with the dumb shit," Pia said.

Abel followed. "So busy you can't even call Zaya back? She's been trying to reach you."

Pia frowned. "What's going on?"

"She wouldn't say, but it sounded serious. She's on her way over."

Pia's stomach twisted. Whatever it was, it wasn't good.

Minutes later, Zaya burst through the door, her usual playful energy absent. Her brown eyes, lined with worry, darted between them.

"It's about Lilliana," she said.

Pia sat up straight. "What about her? Is she okay?"

Zaya exhaled sharply. "No, she's not. Blaze has been putting hands on her."

Pia's heart dropped. "What? Are you serious?"

Zaya nodded. "She FaceTime'd me, trying to cover bruises with makeup before she went home to her mom. Pia, she broke down. She's scared."

Pia felt her blood pressure rise. She knew Blaze was bad news, but this?

Abel, normally joking, was stone-faced. "The best thing to do is go to the police," he said.

Pia exchanged a glance with Zaya. They knew how this worked. The system didn't always protect girls like them.

"We should talk to her together and let her know we're here for her, no matter what. And then we can figure out the best way to help her get out of this situation," Pia stated.

"I'm glad you feel that way," Zaya sighed in relief. "She really needs us right now."

"We need a plan," Pia said, voice firm. "And we need to get Lilliana out."

Zaya nodded. "Tomorrow night. My place. Just us girls."

Pia inhaled deeply. Tomorrow, they would figure this out. But tonight, she was already thinking about the battle ahead.

"I'm free, too?" Abel said.

"Don't you have some random to entertain?" Zaya asked.

"Not this weekend," Abel said smugly.

"Let's just let it be us girls for right now, Abel, but I appreciate your support," Zaya said. "I'll text her now."

"Good, I wonder if she's open to telling her mom?" Pia asked.

"She just texted back and said tomorrow evening was good. Y'all can come over to my house. We can order takeout and talk there. It'll just be us," Zaya said.

"Sounds like a plan to me," Zaya said.

"Well, just keep me posted and let me know how I can help," Abel stated. "Meanwhile, I'm starving now. Let's go get something to eat," Abel said.

"As long as you're treating, I'm eating," Pia laughed.

"With all that government money, you should be treating," Abel combatted.

"Government money?" Zaya repeated, confused.

"Don't listen to him. Just grab your keys. We're riding with you," Pia said, brushing Abel off.

"I'll tell you later," Abel whispered to Zaya as the three headed out the front door.

CHAPTER NINE

Zaya stood in the middle of her bedroom, Mariah Carey's "Always Be My Baby" blasting from the speakers as she twirled dramatically, a pink satin bonnet barely holding onto her head. She clutched a hairbrush, belting out the lyrics like she was performing for the BET Awards.

Lilliana sat cross-legged in front of the mirror, touching up her edges with edge control. Pia, curled up on the bed, scrolled through Connexta, her social feed full of messy comments about last night's shooting.

The trio often enjoyed listening to early 2,000s R&B. The smell of fried rice, sesame chicken, and egg rolls filled the air as they gathered at the dining room table. Zaya, never one to waste time, piled her plate high, talking in between bites.

"You sound terrible," Pia teased, not looking up from her phone.

Zaya placed a dramatic hand on her chest. "Hater. You don't understand real vocals when you hear 'em."

Lilliana snickered but stayed focused on her reflection, adjusting the gold bamboo earrings that dangled from her ears. "Girl, you know she's right. You sound like a cat getting baptized."

Zaya tossed a pillow at Lilliana. "Y'all lack vision. I was in my bag!"

"So what are y'all plans for spring break?" Pia asked, dipping an egg roll into the sweet chili sauce.

"I'm hitting Cancún with some folks from school," Zaya said proudly.

"Wow, that's dope," Pia said.

Lilliana's face tensed, and her fingers fidgeted with her fork.

Zaya gave her a knowing look. "Girl, stop. You know good and well you ain't going nowhere without Blaze."

Lilliana's jaw tightened. "Yes, I am."

But the confidence in her voice faded just as fast as it came.

Pia and Zaya exchanged a glance, their suspicions confirmed.

Then Lilliana muttered, "I gotta watch what I eat, anyway."

Zaya cut her eyes at her. "Watch what? Girl, you built just right."

Pia nodded. "For real. What weight you watching?"

Lilliana hesitated, then shrugged. "I was bloated last week. My hands and feet swelled up so bad. Blaze said—"

She cut herself off, realizing she said too much.

"Blaze, what?" Pia asked.

"Nothing," Lil said as she used her fork to move the food around slowly on her plate.

Zaya put her fork down, voice serious now. "Lil, listen. I called Pia over here because we're worried about you."

Lilliana's eyes flickered with anger, hurt, betrayal. "You told her?!"

"Yes, I did," Zaya said, firm. "Because we love you, and we're not about to sit here and act like everything's cool."

Lilliana pushed back from the table, her eyes wet, jaw clenched. "You had no right."

"Lil, come on," Pia pleaded. "We're just trying to help."

"No," Lilliana snapped. "I told Zaya in confidence. And now you're sitting here, acting all concerned, but let's be real—you don't even like me."

Pia frowned, confused. "What? What are you talking about?"

Lilliana let out a bitter laugh. "Oh, please. We've never been real friends. Zaya's my friend. You're just—there. Always taking up space. Always taking everything."

Pia's chest tightened. "Lil, that's not true," Pia said, confused and visibly hurt.

"Isn't it?" Lilliana challenged. "Remember in sixth grade? When I wanted to go to the Spring Dance with Brandon? But he asked you instead?"

"I didn't even know until after—" Pia started, but Lilliana wasn't finished.

"Ninth grade. Freshman Maid. I ran for it. But somehow, you got nominated—and won."

"I didn't even want it!" Pia exclaimed.

"Then the Sudduth Scholarship," Lilliana spat. "I worked my ass off for that scholarship."

Zaya sighed. "Lil, you're literally rich."

"That's not the point!" Lilliana's voice cracked. "That scholarship was supposed to be mine. It was supposed to prove I could do things on my own, without my mama's money. But you? You always win."

The air in the room felt thick, heavy.

Pia swallowed hard. "Lil, I had no idea you felt this way. I never tried to compete with you."

Lilliana shook her head. "You don't have to try. You just take."

The tension was suffocating. Then, just as suddenly as she exploded, Lilliana grabbed her purse and brushed past Pia, shoulder-checking her.

As she reached the door, she paused. When she turned back, her eyes burned with something deeper than anger.

"I know you're enjoying this," she said, voice low, dangerous. "But I promise you—tables turn."

She slammed the door behind her, leaving a stunned silence.

Zaya exhaled. "Whew. That was not what I expected."

"I know me and Lilliana have never been as close as you two, but. I really thought we were friends. I guess she doesn't like me."

Pia, still frozen in place, shook her head. "I thought we were friends."

Zaya placed a hand on Pia's shoulder. "She's going through something, P. She's hurting, but she'll come around."

Pia wasn't so sure. She sat down, looking distressed.

"Oh, no, no, no! This was supposed to be a girl's night, and it still is. Change of plans. Let's head to Draco's. We're dressed cute enough," Zaya said, smiling. Girls' night out."

"Girl, I'm not in the mood to go out," Pia contested.

"Music, good vibes, good-looking guys, let's gooo!!!! It'll take your mind off of Lil...at least for a moment. When's the last time you had a night out? I'll even call Abel. I know he's down," said Zaya.

With an eye roll, Pia got up and grabbed her purse.

"Yessssssssssss!" Zaya cheered.

The nightclub pulsed with energy, a blend of flashing lights and thumping bass that reverberated through the packed room while the latest hip hop hits permeated the building. Draco's was the town's hot spot for clubbing. The smell of cologne, liquor, and hookah smoke clung to the air. The neon lights bounced off jewelry, acrylic nails, and designer fits.[1]

Pia threaded her way through the crowd, her eyes scanning the scene. It didn't take long for her to spot Abel. He was dressed in

---

1. **Book Soundtrack Cue**: "Essence" – Wizkid ft. Tems.

a black designer Polo with black jeans, Jordan Retros 3s, and his usual cocky grin. He waved her and Zaya over to a sectional.

"How'd you get a section so fast?" Zaya asked.

"You know I'm the man in this place. I get anything I want," Abel bragged.

"Boy, please," Pia snorted.

"I'll be back," Abel said as he bee-lined for a girl in the corner, showing more skin than fabric.

"I'm thirsty. You want a drink?" Pia asked.

"You got an ID?" Zaya returned the question.

"No, I just want a Sprite, no alcohol," Pia said.

"Get me one, too. I'll hold the section down until Romeo gets back," Zaya said.

Pia headed toward the bar. As she approached the counter, she found an empty stool and sat down, signaling the bartender for a drink.

"Is this seat taken?" the guy asked.

Pia looked up to see a strikingly handsome man standing next to her. His smile was the first thing she noticed. His teeth were perfect, and he had one dimple in his left cheek. His gray eyes wore a smile, too. Every inch of him was tanned very well. The guy stood about 5'11", the perfect height for an embrace. He wore a tailored blazer with brown jeans. His confident demeanor set him apart from the crowd.

Pia tilted her head, intrigued. "Not anymore."

"I'm Nolan, by the way."

"Pia," she introduced herself, shaking his outstretched hand. His grip was firm, yet his touch was warm.

"So, Pia," Nolan began, "what brings you to Draco's tonight?"

Pia shrugged lightly, grabbing the two drinks as the bartender set them down. "Just hanging with some friends. How about you?"

"Pretty much the same. I'm a realtor, so it's always busy. But tonight, I decided to let loose a bit," Nolan said.

"A realtor, huh?" Pia said, raising an eyebrow. "That sounds interesting."

"It has its moments," Nolan admitted, leaning in slightly. "But enough about me. What do you do, Pia?"

"I'm a dance student and dance instructor," she replied, noting the surprise flicker in his eyes.

"Wow, no wonder you look amazing," Nolan said, genuinely impressed.

Pia blushed, nodding. "It's a lot of fun."

Nolan's gaze lingered on her for a moment, his smile widening.

"I would love to see you dance," he said.

"I would love for you to watch," Pia said, leaning in closer, feeling an unexpected connection with this charming stranger. "But right now, I have to get back to my friends."

"I have a feeling this is just the beginning of our story," Nolan remarked.

Pia felt a flutter in her chest, a mixture of excitement and anticipation. "I think you're right, Nolan. Take my number."

With that, Pia rattled off her number as Nolan saved it in his phone. Pia's eyes caught sight of a tattoo peeking out from under Nolan's sleeve. It was an intricate design, a combination of symbols that seemed familiar.

"That's an interesting tattoo," Pia remarked, curiosity piqued. "What does it mean?"

Nolan glanced at his arm, then back at Pia, his smile turning a bit more thoughtful. "Ah, this," he said, lightly tracing the tattoo with his fingers. "It's the square and compasses. I'm a member of the Masonic Lodge."

"Oh, there's actually one across from my dance studio," Pia said. "On Belvedere."

"Small world. I attend that one," Nolan said, grinning.

"I guess I'll be seeing you around," Pia said with a flicker in her eyes.

She moved gracefully through the crowd, careful not to drop the drinks.

"P! I almost forgot to tell y'all Lilliana is here, too. She's with Blaze over by the DJ booth."

"That's cool. We came to have fun. We can deal with her at another time," Pia said.

The three danced, sang, and laughed until it was almost 2 am.

"Hey, where did y'all park?" Abel said as they made it outside.

"We're right across the street. What about you?" Zaya asked.

"I parked on the side, but I'll walk y'all to the jeep first," Abel said.

The parking lot was full of people not ready to go home. Music blared through car windows and you could hear chatter throughout the parking lot. Cars swerved up and down the aisles sequentially.

"We're right there," Pia pointed at the jeep 15 yards away from them.

Gunshots began to ring out across the parking lot. As people ran and ducked down, one girl fell on top of Pia, who had tried to slide beneath a car. Pia's muffled screams caught Abel's attention, who immediately pulled her away from under the girl. They all stayed down until the gunshots stopped.

People began to jump in their cars and speed away from the club. Abel grabbed Pia and Zaya's hands, and they ran to the jeep.

"They killed him! He's dead!" a girl screamed a few feet from the jeep. A crowd began to grow in that area. The screams and cries filled the air as sirens grew near.

"That was Blaze!" Abel said, short of breath.

"What? Are you sure?" Zaya asked.

"Yeah, when the shooting first started, I caught a glimpse of him in the passenger seat of a black Tahoe. He was one of the shooters," Abel said.

"What about Lilliana? Did you see her?" Zaya asked.

"No, I didn't."

"Okay, well, we're headed home. Text us when you make it," Zaya said.

"Aight, y'all be safe," Abel said and began a slow jog to his car.

CHAPTER TEN

P ia woke up to the sound of her phone vibrating against the nightstand. She groaned, eyes barely open, and reached for it. A notification from Nolan lit up the screen.

> Nolan: *Hey, just checking on you. I heard about the shooting last night. Were you still there when it happened?*

Pia rubbed her eyes, a small smile tugging at her lips. Handsome and thoughtful.

She stretched, her body sore from dancing, and was about to reply when another knock sounded at her bedroom door.

"Hey, sweet pea, you up?" Pierre called from the hallway.

"Yeah, dad, I just woke up," she responded. "Come in."

"I didn't hear you come in last night. Did you have fun with your friends?" Pierre asked. He was dressed up in a gray suit, with a blue button up and black dress shoes. Although you could see his age, Pia smiled at her good-looking dad. He cleaned up well.

"My night was fine, dad. What I want to know is where are you going looking like somebody's deacon?" Pia inquired.

"Rosa, I mean Ms. Jimenez, invited me to church," Pierre said nervously.

Pia raised an eyebrow. "Ms. Jimenez? As in Lilliana's mom?"

He scratched the back of his head. "Yeah. She invited both of us, but I figured you might be too tired to go."

"You figured right," Pia chuckled, pulling the covers around her tighter. "Besides, you know I like my sermons like I like my shopping: online."

"You new-age kids are something else. So...you sure you're okay with this?"

Pierre asked nervously.

Pia pulled the blanket down, giving him a knowing look. "Dad, I don't care if you're dating Ms. Jimenez."

Pierre coughed. "I never said—"

"Dad." Pia crossed her arms.

Pierre sighed, smiling sheepishly. "Alright, fine. I like her. She's a good woman."

Pia shrugged. "Then go to church and enjoy your Sunday, Reverend Pierre."

Her father laughed, shaking his head as he walked out. "You got jokes. Well, maybe one day you and Lilliana could join us," Pierre smiled.

"Maybe," Pia said. "I think it's nice that Ms. Jimenez invited you to church. I hope it's a great sermon. I'll see you when you get back," Pia said.

"Okay, enjoy your rest," Pierre said as walked out of the room.

Just as Pia grabbed her phone to respond to Nolan, another text came through.

Ms. Marie: You're late.

"Oh, shit!" Pia rushed to get dressed and head to the studio.

Twenty minutes and a half bath later, Pia pulled into the studio parking lot. Jumping out of the car with black tights, a white tank top, and a Nike baseball cap, she glanced down to open the door as Ms. Marie stood by glaring at her. They both went inside and locked the door.

"Pia," Ms. Marie said.

Pia was moving around quickly, turning on all of the lights.

"Stop and look at me," Ms. Marie said firmly.

Pia stopped and slowly brought her eyes to meet Ms. Marie's, whose arms were folded, folded her arms, the gold bracelets on her wrist clinking softly.

"Time is the most precious thing we have," Ms. Marie said. "I don't take it kindly when mine is wasted."

"Yes, ma'am," Pia said quietly.

"So, why are you late?" Ms. Marie asked.

Pia sat down in a nearby foldable chair. She pulled her cap off and tugged at her tight coils.

"I overslept," Pia said.

Ms. Marie arched an eyebrow. "Why?"

Pia hesitated. "Last night was... a lot."

Ms. Marie pulled up a chair, sitting with her back straight. "Go on."

Pia exhaled. "I got into an argument with Lilliana—turns out, she's been secretly hating me for years. Then, we went to the club to blow off steam, and a shooting broke out in the parking lot."

"Mm-hmm," Ms. Marie said. "Is that all?"

"Yes, that's it," Pia said.

"I understand," Ms. Marie said.

Ms. Marie was silent for a beat, then asked, "What happened when the shooting started?"

Pia frowned. "What do you mean?"

"Did you try to use your powers?"

Pia's stomach tightened. "I did. And nothing happened."

Ms. Marie leaned forward. "Tell me exactly what you felt."

Pia thought back. "At first, panic. Then shock, fear, and then... suffocated."

Ms. Marie nodded. "When you used your power in the river, you weren't thinking about it. It was instinct. But now that you're aware of it, your mind is getting in the way."

Pia sighed. "But how can I focus when bullets are flying?"

"You'll need to train yourself to use your power under pressure." Ms. Marie's voice was calm, but firm. "You think that was the last time you'll be in danger?"

Pia looked away.

"Three dead in the last week. 103 homicides this year—and it's not even summer yet." Ms. Marie held Pia's gaze. "You need to be ready."

Pia straightened up. "Then I need more intense training."

"Back it up to the friend," Ms. Marie said thinking, as she walked to the chair near Pia and slid it around to sit directly facing her. She sat with her back straight and hands resting beside her.

"Her name is Lilliana, Lilliana Jimenez. For some reason, she seems to think that I intentionally do things to hurt her, but I would never..." Pia's voice trailed off.

"I see. Pia, jealousy can be dangerous. Be sure to keep an eye out for that one," Ms. Maried said.

"I will," Pia said.

Ms. Marie smiled slightly. "Good. Close the blinds—we're getting started."[1]

As Pia turned to do so, a knock sounded at the door.

She peeked through the glass and saw Raymond Windham—the older man who attended the Masonic Lodge across from the studio.

---

1. **Book Soundtrack Cue:** "The King's Affirmation"–Iniko.

Pia cracked the door. "Good afternoon."

Raymond tipped his hat. "Afternoon, young lady. Just came by to say hello. Am I interrupting something?"

Pia hesitated, glancing back at Ms. Marie. "Actually, yes. I have a private lesson."

Raymond chuckled. "Understood. You ladies have a good day."

Pia shut the door and locked it, turning back to Ms. Marie.

Ms. Marie was watching Raymond through the blinds. "Do you know that man?"

"Not really," Pia said. "I met him during the ice storm, but I never saw him before that."

Ms. Marie hummed in thought. "Interesting."

Pia could tell Ms. Marie was in thought as she stood quietly for a moment.

"Okay, let's get to it. We've worked on healing, force fields, and energy blasts, which still need some work. Today, I want to teach you how to use your strength," Ms. Marie said.

Pia's eyes lit up. "For real?"

Ms. Marie nodded. "Your strength is a gift, but if you can't control it, it's a problem."

She pulled out a small, smooth stone and set it on the table. "Lift this. Not with all your might—just enough."

Pia picked up the stone, feeling its solid weight in her palm.

"Good," Ms. Marie said. "Now, let's level up."

She led Pia to the corner of the studio where a 5-foot speaker stood. "Lift this. Slowly."

Pia crouched, gripped the speaker, and lifted it with ease.

Ms. Marie smiled. "Good. Now—don't let it overwhelm you."

Pia held the weight steady, feeling her power flow through her. Her arms trembled slightly, but she kept control.

She gently lowered it back to the ground, a proud grin spreading across her face.

Ms. Marie nodded. "That speaker is about 100 pounds. Now—" her eyes darted across the room—"let's take it up a notch."

Pia followed her gaze, and her eyes widened.

"Ms. Marie. You want me to lift the vending machine?!"

Ms. Marie smirked. "Unplug it first."

Pia sighed, unplugged it, and crouched. Do not let it overwhelm you.

With a deep breath, she tapped into her power and lifted the vending machine clear off the ground.

"Bravo!" Ms. Marie clapped.

Pia eased the machine back down and smiled at her accomplishment, feeling stronger than ever.

"That's all the time I have for today. I know we need to work on those energy blasts, so the next time we'll meet at my place," Ms. Marie said.

"Where's Tay?" Pia asked, just realizing his absence. She's never known him not to be with Ms. Marie.

"Tay is fine. He's with a friend," Ms. Marie said. "Come. Let's get out of here so I can get back to him."

The two walked out and noticed Raymond leaning against the passenger side of a black four-door Lincoln across the street. As they looked in his direction, he waved with a big smile. He was talking to someone sitting inside the car.

"He always around?" Ms. Marie asked.

Pia hesitated. "Lately, yeah."

Ms. Marie walked Pia to her car. "Tay and I have to take a trip. We'll be gone for about a week. I'll let you know when I return, so we can work on those energy blasts."

"Okay, got it."

Ms. Marie's voice dropped. "Be careful, Pia. Of your surround-ings—and your company."

Pia swallowed. "Yes, ma'am."

CHAPTER ELEVEN

Raymond sat on a worn-out brown leather chair inside his office at the Masonic Lodge, tapping his pen on the oak wood desk. His eyes flicked across the glowing screen of his news app on Connexta, scrolling through the latest headlines. He pulled back the blinds—rows of dark green vehicles lined the street, their heavy tires grinding against the pavement. Soldiers poured out, their boots thudding like a slow, rolling drumbeat of war. A knock on the door broke his trance.

"Come in," he answered fervently.

The door swung open, revealing General George Beaumont, his uncle—a man whose presence alone could silence a room. His thin, almost translucent skin was creased with lines of experience, his short-cropped gray hair the only indication of his age. Midnight blue slacks with a gold braid denoted his rank, his chest decorated with service medals that glinted under the office light.

"Nephew! It's good to see you. You're looking more and more like your father every day," George greeted, stepping forward with an outstretched hand.

"Yes, sir. I wish he was still here. I sure do miss the old man," Raymond said.

"I do, too," George said, his voice weighted with memory. "But the work we're doing now—this mission—it'll bring justice. For him. For all of us."

"I didn't think they'd send the military here so soon," Raymond exhaled.

"Yeah, things are escalating faster than expected. Orders from the top came in last night. Top brass want a heavy presence in all key locations," George said in an earnest tone.

"How long do we have?" Raymond asked anxiously.

"A few days, maybe a week. Officially, they're saying it's for maintenance and upgrades, but you know...," George said.

"So, this is definitely a key location? Windsorville?" Raymond asked uncertainly.

"More than that," George confirmed. "It's a hotspot. The government's afraid that if they organize, they'll pose a significant threat."

"Understood," Raymond said. "We have everything set up for your men."

"Good." George clapped his shoulder. "That's why I trust you, son. You've always been a good soldier." He took a measured step back. "Now, tell me—what do we have on Rhema Brown?"

"Have a seat," Raymond sighed as he motioned at the couch in his office. "You should have a few minutes to catch up while the soldiers get settled, right?" Raymond asked.

George lowered himself onto the edge of the couch, back straight, hands clasped. Raymond sat beside him, tension thickening between them.

"Listen, I know that you've been briefed, but I need you to understand the gravity of what's going on."

"I'm listening," Raymond said with an uneasiness in his tone.

General George closes his eyes briefly, then exhales deeply, turning to face his nephew.

George exhaled deeply, his face unreadable. "This is personal." He hesitated, then met Raymond's gaze. "You were told your father died in the line of duty."

Raymond nodded stiffly.

"But that's not the whole truth."

A beat passed. Then another.

George continued, his voice a low, steady force. "Your father was killed by one of them. A Nuru."

Raymond's jaw tightened. "What?"

George pulled out an old, frayed document from his portfolio and handed it over. Raymond's eyes scanned the faded writing.

Robert Beaumont was investigating a series of strange deaths. Unnatural. No logical explanation. All linked to a man—no, a being—who could control energy. The locals called him 'Nuru.'

Raymond's breath hitched. "Nuru?"

George nodded grimly. "Your father was close to uncovering the truth. Too close."

Raymond's grip on the paper tightened as his uncle spoke.

"The night it happened, your dad and his deputy were en route to pick him up. The Nuru resisted. Your father tried to restrain him." George paused, his face darkening. "The deputy saw it happen. Said the Nuru formed a ball of light—pure energy—and hurled it at your father. Killed him instantly. The deputy barely escaped with a wound to his leg."[1]

Silence hung between them.

Raymond rose abruptly, his chest heaving. "Why did you keep this from me?"

"For twenty years?"

George nodded solemnly. "With your father gone, and you being a Mason, it's time you knew the truth. This isn't just Windsorville anymore. Homeland Security has mapped out hotspots across the country. People with these supernatural abilities—they don't just defy nature, they defy order."

He pulled out a tablet, tapped the screen, and turned it toward Raymond. A video played. A man lifting a car with one hand, eyes glowing like embers. With a flick of his wrist, he hurled it against a wall. The impact shook the screen.

Raymond's eyes widened at the footage.

"Strength beyond physics," George murmured. "Control over energy. The ability to kill with a stroke of the hand. What happens if they decide they want more? More power? More control?"

---

1. **Book Soundtrack Cue**: "Not Afraid" – Eminem.

Raymond shook his head, still processing everything. His father had been investigating something far darker than he had ever imagined. And now, that darkness seemed to have found him, too.

"I know you're upset, but that's why we have to prove that Rhema Brown is a Nuru and capture her before she can kill anyone," the general explained.

Raymond swallowed hard. "Are all of them dangerous?"

"We can't tell who's safe and who isn't. Not until it's too late." George tapped the screen again. Another video. A ruined city. Buildings crumbling. Smoke rising. In the distance, a figure hovered mid-air, glowing with raw, untamed energy.

"The government won't take chances. If they let them operate freely, it would be chaos. We'd have a war on our hands," George said.

Raymond's mind whirled. His father's death. The secret war. The Nurus. And now, the woman they were after—Rhema Brown.

"Think about it: strength that defies physics, control over energy, the ability to kill with a stroke of the hand. They have the ability to rewrite the rules of the world, and not in ways we can predict or control," general george said.

What will the government do? Lock them all up?

George gets closer, his voice dropping, heavy with the weight of the truth.

"No, it's not that simple. They don't want to imprison everyone with powers. But they want to control them. Monitor them. If these individuals were allowed to operate freely, it would be chaos. Nations wouldn't trust each other. Governments would collapse out of fear. And most of all... it would become a war between those who have power and those who don't. Those who could not be controlled would be exterminated."

Raymond's eyes meet his uncle's, understanding dawning in the silence. This wasn't just about others with powers. This was about him, too.

"I have to report back to Alexander Franklinton within 48 hours. He's the Secretary of Homeland Security. I trust that you will help us get what we need on Rhema Brown by then?"

"Not a problem," Raymond said with a renewed conviction.

He needed answers. And if Rhema Brown was one of them, he would get them—no matter what it took.

Raymond stepped outside. The setting sun cast long shadows over the military trucks. Soldiers moved methodically, securing the perimeter. His thoughts raced.

Then he saw her.

Pia Pierce stood outside her shop, arms folded, staring at the trucks with keen, wary eyes.

Raymond narrowed his gaze.

What business do you have with that old woman, Pia? He thought. *I'll find out soon enough.*

CHAPTER
TWELVE

"Eya! Eya! Toma, ren! Ren!" recited Lilliana.

The air in Lilliana's room was thick with the scent of burning sage and incense. Shadows flicker against the walls, dancing with the flame of the single candle illuminating the room. On a small wooden table, a collection of items is carefully arranged: an old photograph of Pia, a blackened jar filled with mysterious herbs and oils, and a crude doll made of cloth and string. The room hums with a dark, ominous energy.

Lilliana sat cross-legged on the floor, her face illuminated by the candle's flicker, her eyes narrowed with focus. She muttered under her breath, the words a mixture of French and English, taught to her by her cousin from New Orleans. A small, worn book lay open beside her, its pages yellowed and covered in handwritten notes passed down through generations. Her fingers, now trembling slightly, grasped the doll she's crafted to resemble Pia.

"Pia," she whispered, rolling the name across her tongue as if tasting something bitter. "You always thought you were better than me. You think you can get away with everything, don't you?" Her voice was sharp and low.

She adjusted the tiny scrap of cloth tied around the doll's waist, ensuring it resembled Pia as much as possible. With a deep breath, she reached for a long silver pin beside the doll, her hand steadying as she lifted it up. She glanced at the photograph of Pia, her old friend—now enemy—smiling innocently. Lilliana's lips curled into a bitter smile. A voice echoed in her memory—her cousin's from New Orleans, instructing her as a child.

"You should have never thought you were better than me," she muttered. "I'll show you."

She leaned closer to the doll; the pin hovering above its chest. Her cousin's voice echoes in her mind: "Intent, Lilliana. It's all about intent. Feel it. See it. Believe it." Her hand steadied as she began to focus, eyes locked on the doll.

Her grip tightened. "I hope you feel every bit of what you've done to me. Puedes arder para siempre!"

She drove the pin into the doll's chest, twisting it slowly, her eyes dancing with excitement. The candle flickers violently, casting eerie shadows on the walls. The air seems to thicken around her, as if the very room was holding its breath.

A sudden knock at the door, loud and jarring, shattered the trance.

Lilliana gasped, her hand jerking, the pin clattering to the floor. The room's energy shifted in an instant, the candlelight steadying, as if the house itself had exhaled.

Her chest heaving, she looks at the door, then back at the doll in her hand, unsure whether she's succeeded. She throws the doll and the book underneath her bed, and she quickly blows out the candles.

"Come in," she called out, her voice just shy of steady.

"Girl, why are you sitting in the dark?" Zaya says as she entered the room and turned on the lights. "It smells like you've been burning incense."

"Well, I like to burn sage and incense to get rid of negative spirits that may come around me," Lilliana said.

Zaya flopped onto the bed. "I hope you're not saying I got bad energy."

"Not you," Lilliana muttered. "Spirits transfer, so you have to be careful of the company you keep," Lilliana said with a sneer.

Zaya sighed, rubbing her temples. "You still mad about Pia?"

"I was never *not* mad about Pia." Lilliana's voice sharpened, her gaze darkening. "I tolerated her because of you. But I'm not doing that anymore."[1]

Zaya hesitated. "Lil, she's not that bad."

"She's fake," Lilliana snapped. "You can be friends with her, but don't expect me to be around."

Zaya's shoulders tensed. "That puts me in a tight spot."

"I feel like I'm being forced to choose," Zaya fussed.

"I don't care what you choose. Just keep that bitch away from me."

There was a pause. The tension thickened by the incense and sage.

Lilliana softened, her voice dropping. "Look, I know you mean well. You've always been a good friend. But I can't pretend with people anymore. You don't know what it's like to be treated like an afterthought."

Zaya frowned. "That's not fair."

Lilliana's mask slipped for a moment. "You ever feel so alone that even your thoughts turn against you? That's me, Zaya. Every damn day."

Zaya's expression shifted, her eyes welling. "Lil..."

---

1. **Book Soundtrack Cue**: "Let the Beat Build" – Lil Wayne.

"I've thought about ending it so many times, but you—you always pull me back." Lilliana exhaled sharply. "So, yeah. I need you in my life. But I don't need her."

Zaya reached out, squeezing her hand. "I'll always be here for you. But promise me—if you ever feel that way again, you'll talk to me first."

Lilliana nodded, swallowing past the lump in her throat. "I promise."

Across town, Pia lay sprawled on her bed, phone pressed to her ear, a lazy smile on her lips.

"Good morning, beautiful."

Nolan's voice was smooth, rich like a Sunday morning jazz tune.

"Good morning, handsome," Pia murmured, feeling heat rise to her cheeks.

"What's your weekend looking like?"

Pia sighed. "Busy. I've got school deadlines, and I need to catch up on work."

Nolan chuckled. "Work, huh? Too busy for a handsome guy like me?"

"You do have a nice face," Pia teased. "But yeah, the timing's off."

"That's what you think now," Nolan said, his voice dropping into something softer, more certain. "One day, I'm going to ask at the perfect time, and you'll wish you'd said yes sooner."

Pia laughed. "Oh, really?"

"Mm-hmm."

She bit her lip, the warmth in his voice wrapping around her like a slow embrace. But before she could reply, another call beeped in. Zaya.

"Hey, I gotta go. Talk soon?"

"You better."

Pia clicked over. "Hey, girl. What's up?"

Zaya's voice was tight. "Just left Lilliana's."

Pia groaned. "Oh, here we go."

"Don't start," Zaya warned. "Lil's been through a lot. You don't have to like her, but don't act like she's had it easy."

Pia rolled her eyes. "Being rich and spoiled is hard, huh?"

Zaya's tone sharpened. "That's not fair. Just because someone has money doesn't mean they don't suffer. That doesn't mean she's immune from dealing with real life shit, Pia."

"I hear ya," Pia said sarcastically.

"I'm serious, P."

"Whatever."

"You know what? Maybe Lil was right about you."

Pia sat up. "Excuse me?"

"I need some space," Zaya muttered before hanging up.

Pia stared at her phone, stunned. A knot formed in her stomach. Zaya was her *best friend*. Had she really just lost her over *Lilliana*?

Pia threw her phone down and sat on the bed, taking in deep breaths. Zaya was her best friend. They rarely ever had a serious disagreement. *But what the hell just happened?* Pia laid across her bed, replaying the conversation.

Before she could dwell on it, a sharp tapping at her window startled her.

Tap, tap, tap, tap, tap, tap.

Pia's heart pounded as she pulled back the curtain. Abel stood outside, grinning.

"Damn, P. I've been knocking forever."

"I'm coming," Pia said.

Pia turned on the living room lights and unlocked the door. "Sorry. Long day."

Abel settled onto the couch, scrolling through his phone. "So, guess what?"

"Let me guess. Girl problems?" she inquired.

"I'm juggling like three different women right now, and it's... it's a mess. Anyways, this is wilder. You ever hear about the internet blackout theory?"

Pia frowned. "What now?"

"Connexta's been blowing up. Some folks are saying the government's about to shut the whole internet down for, like, weeks. Something about controlling information before a major event."

Pia raised an eyebrow. "And you believe that?"

Abel shrugged. "People are stockpiling food, batteries, the whole nine. Could be real."

"Or it could be another conspiracy theory."

"Maybe." Abel leaned back. "But what if it's not?"

A strange chill ran down Pia's spine. Between Blaze, Lilliana, and now *this*—something in the air felt different. Like the whole world was shifting beneath her feet, and she hadn't quite found her balance yet.

She just hoped she'd land on solid ground before it was too late.

"My turn," Pia said.

"What's up?" Abel said, intrigued.

"Soo...Zaya calls me."

"And..."

"And she was taking up for Lilliana, but I wasn't trying to hear it. The conversation got heated and I think I just lost my friend," Pia said as her eyes became glossy.

Abel pulled Pia close to him and wrapped his arms around her.

"Well, you'll always have me as your friend," Abel said in a low breath.

"Thank you, but unhand me now," Pia said.

Abel sat back on the couch with a grin.

"What?! I can't console you."

"Boy, you play too much. I'm being serious and you're trying to take advantage of my vulnerability," she said, punching him in the arm.

"Pia, seriously, have you been lifting weights?" he said, rubbing his arm.

"What do I do about Zaya?" Pia groaned.

"Give her some time. I'm sure it's no fun being stuck between two friends," Abel said.

"Yeah, you're right. I just hope we can work things out," Pia sighed.

"I hope so, too, P."

CHAPTER THIRTEEN

The moon hung low over Windsorville, its silver glow casting long shadows along the quiet streets. Pia locked up her dance studio, exhaling sharply as the weight of the evening settled over her. Her body ached from training, but her mind was restless with thoughts of Zaya, Lilliana, and the strange energy she'd felt earlier swirling together like an unfinished rhythm.

"Great job, Pia. You're gaining control over your powers," Marie said as the pair walked to the studio door.

Pia beamed at Ms. Marie, acknowledging her progress. "Thank you," she said, relieved.

"Tomorrow, my place," Ms. Marie said as she headed to her car.

"I'll be there."

Pia went back inside the studio and closed the door. As Pia grabbed her bag and turned toward the door, she froze. Someone was standing in the middle of the studio floor.

"Blaze?" Pia asked.

Blaze stood there with his arms crossed, head tilted just slightly. His tall, broad frame was dressed in a black t-shirt and black jean pants. His eyes were menacing, fixed on her with a quiet intensity that made the hairs on the back of her neck stand up. His energy was thick with something dangerous.[1]

He began walking toward her with the heavy, deliberate steps of someone used to being feared.

"Yo," he said, his voice low and rough, "we gotta talk."

Pia's pulse quickened, but she squared her shoulders. She stood her ground, one hand tightening around the strap of her bag.

"Talk about what?"

Blaze stopped a few feet in front of her, close enough that she could see the faded scars lining his knuckles, his hands flexing at his sides. "Lilliana."

Pia's heart skipped a beat, but she kept her expression steady. "This is about Lilliana?"

---

1. **Book Soundtrack Cue**: "Power" – Kanye West.

"She's upset," Blaze continued. "You know how that makes me feel?"

Pia clenched her jaw. "I didn't do anything to her."

Blaze's jaw tightened, his eyes narrowing. "You think you can just run your mouth, make her feel some kinda way, and nothing's gonna happen?"

Pia took a breath, trying to stay calm. "I didn't mean to upset her, Blaze. Whatever happened, it wasn't intentional."

Blaze let out a short, humorless laugh. "You think I care if it was intentional or not?"

He took a step closer, towering over her now, his voice a low growl. "When you mess with her, you mess with me. And that's a problem, Pia."

Pia's stomach twisted in knots, but she lifted her chin, refusing to show fear. "I don't want any trouble. Lilliana's my friend too, Blaze. If I upset her, I'll talk to her, fix it."

Blaze shook his head, a dangerous glint in his eyes. "You don't get it. This ain't about talking. You hurt her, you hurt me. And I don't let people get away with that."

The threat hung heavy in the air between them, but Pia didn't back down. "I'm not scared of you, Blaze."

Blaze smirked, leaning in so close she could feel the heat of his breath. "You should be."

"Yeah, that can't be worse than what you do to her," Pia said without thinking.

Blaze smirked, then, faster than she could react, lunged. His hand wrapped around her throat, pressing her against the wall.

Pia stood there struggling, her body tense, her mind racing. Her legs kicked rapidly as she tried to break his hold.

"*Focus, Pia, focus!*" she thought to herself.

"Hey! Get off her!" A loud voice cut through the tension.

Blaze turned to see who had entered the studio without letting Pia go.

Raymond stood in the doorway, his expression unreadable.

"Man, who the hell are you?"

Raymond didn't answer. Instead, he moved fast, shoving Blaze back. Pia fell to her knees, clutching her throat, struggling to steady her breath.

"You okay?" Raymond asked, standing over Pia.

Pia looked up at Raymond and nodded weakly, but her gaze flicked past him, her eyes widening by the second.

130

Raymond turned to see a gun pointed in his face.

"You should've been minding your own business, old man," Blaze said and cocked the gun.

Before the shot rang out, something inside Pia snapped. A surge of energy pulsed through her veins, hot and urgent. The room crackled as a green-glowing orb formed around Raymond, shimmering like a force field.

The bullet hit the barrier and disintegrated mid-air.

The air around Pia shifted. Time seemed to slow. Blaze turned the gun toward her, but she was already moving. Her body knew before her mind did—she grabbed his arm and, with an effortless motion, hurled him across the studio. He slammed into the far wall with a sickening thud.

The glow around Raymond flickered before vanishing. He turned to Pia, his face a mixture of shock and something else—fear?

Pia's breath was ragged. "Adrenaline," she lied, forcing a nervous chuckle. "I guess I'm stronger than I look."

"Not that. The bullet. The green bubble. How did you do *that*?" Raymond stressed, eyes wild with disbelief.

Pia hesitated. "Can we keep this between us?"

Raymond studied her for a long moment, then exhaled. "You saved my life. I owe you that much."

Relief washed over her.

"Thank you," Pia said with a sigh. "So, what do we do about him? Should I call the police?"

Blaze groaned from across the room, barely conscious. Raymond walked over to Blaze and checked his pulse.

"He's still breathing. Let's not get the police involved. Let me handle this."

Pia wasn't sure what that meant, but she nodded.

She picked up her bag, pulling out her phone and texting Nolan:

> Wyd?

Nothing, thinking about you

> The worst thing just happened!

What???

> This guy attacked me at my dance studio.

WTF, are you ok???

Yes, I'm okay. One of the masons came just in time.

Do I need to come?

No, no, it's fine now. I'm just a bit shaken. That's all. I'm getting ready to leave now.

Which mason was it? That came over?

This guy named Raymond.

Okay, I could still come if you want me to.

No, I'll be home before you could even make it here.

Okay, let me know when you make it home.

"So, what are you going to do with him?" Pia asked as she locked the studio door from the outside.

"We're going to put him back in his car and drive him far away from here," Raymond said. "Get home safe."

"Will do, and thanks again for your help tonight," Pia said. She turned and walked to her car while her stomach flipped violently. Once she pulled off and was out of earshot, she called Ms. Marie.

"Yes, child?" Ms. Marie answered.

"Something just happened," Pia said nervously.

"Come, now," Ms. Marie said.

The line went dead.

Pia stood at the foot of the sprawling mansion, its white pillars towering over her like ancient sentinels guarding secrets long kept. Spanish moss dripped from the ancient oaks surrounding the estate, swaying gently in the nighttime breeze as if whispering their own stories. The air crackled with energy, an almost tangible force she could feel beneath her skin—a hum that resonated in her bones.

The moment Pia stepped onto the porch, she felt it. The energy. Like the house itself was alive, watching, waiting. She can't recall sensing this energy before. She reached for the door, only for it to open on its own with a slow, deliberate groan, welcoming her inside.

The door opened before she could knock.

Ms. Marie and sat in the parlor, her piercing eyes never missing a beat. Her hair twisted into an elegant knot, her dress flowing like water over the ornate chair. Her presence was commanding, and Pia could feel the gravity of her power swirling around her like a silent storm.

Tay sat near her, smiling and giggling as if he played with an entity right in front of him.

"You're late, child," Ms. Marie said, her voice soft yet firm.

"Well, traffic was-" Pia started.

"What happened?" Ms. Marie interrupted.

Pia hesitated, the words forming in her mind before she found the courage to speak.

"Raymond saw... saw me use my powers," she said quietly.

Ms. Marie's eyes narrowed, shifting from one side of the room to the other.

Ms. Marie's gaze darkened. "How?"

Pia told her everything—Blaze, the attack, the bullet, the barrier. The words tumbled out in a rush. When she finished, the room felt heavier.

Ms. Marie sighed. "Raymond is not who you think he is."

Pia frowned. "What do you mean?"

Pia's stomach tightened, and her eyes widened. This danger seemed more real than what she experienced earlier with Blaze. The air seemed to grow heavier around her, pressing in, demanding her to understand the gravity of what she'd just learned.

Before Pia could respond, a strange sensation rippled through the room. The house seemed to exhale, and Pia felt a new kind of energy washing over her—one that was different, deeper, and more intense.

And then she saw Tay standing up from his seat.

His head tilted slightly as though he were listening to something far away. The house itself seemed to speak to him, every sound a subtle communication.

The floorboards creaked rhythmically beneath his feet, and Pia realized they weren't just making noise—they were speaking to him, guiding him. He stopped in the center of the room, his head tilting slightly toward Pia as if he could sense her gaze.

"He's telling you it's going to be okay, child. He listens in ways you and I cannot," Ms. Marie said softly, watching Pia's reaction.

"Tay's power is tied to the energy of the earth, to the house itself. He hears what we don't, sees what we can't."

Pia watched Tay, mesmerized. His calmness soothed her.

"We are working on a way to deal with this problem. As for Raymond, you saved his life, did you not?"

"Yes, I did," Pia answered.

"He may not be so quick to turn you in, but keep your distance. From now on, we'll only practice here. When you go to the studio, get in and out. Never stay late by yourself."

"Okay, got it. But did I hear you say you met with *other Nurus*?"

"Yes, and you'll meet them soon enough. Ms. Marie met her eyes. "You are stepping into something bigger than you know."

Pia shivered. Deep down, she already knew that much was true.

CHAPTER FOURTEEN

"**M**an, I am ready to smash!" Abel said as he jumped out of Pia's car, stretching his arms like he was preparing for battle.

The sun was high, the 80-degree breeze carrying the smell of fried catfish and cornbread from Collin's Kitchen. Pia wore ripped jean shorts, a fitted yellow crop top, and white Air Jordan 1s. Abel sported faded, distressed black jeans, a black tee, black Air Force Ones, and had a smirk that screamed trouble. Pia was enjoying his company this past week, even though she yearned to pick up the phone and call Zaya.

"I'm starving too," Pia grinned, doing a little two-step before they stepped inside.

The restaurant buzzed with the energy of the lunch rush. The scent of Cajun spice and slow-cooked greens hit them as they ordered their food. There were barely any empty seats, but Abel found a table near the rear of the restaurant.

It didn't take long for the food to come out. As soon as their plates hit the table, all conversation ceased. Fried chicken, catfish, greens, mac and cheese, cornbread—it was a feast. For the first five minutes, the only sounds were their forks scraping and the occasional grunt of approval.

"This place don't miss," Abel mumbled between bites.

"Ever," Pia agreed, while mixing her greens and cornbread.

Then the mood shifted. Pia looked up and locked eyes with Zaya, who was entering the restaurant and headed to the to-go counter. Zaya quickly looked away as if she didn't see Pia.

"She didn't even speak," Pia muttered, dropping her fork on the plate.

"Who?" Abel said, still chewing without looking up.

"Zaya. She's here, and she looked right at me!"

"Maybe she really didn't see you."

"Don't make excuses for her. Let's go," Pia's jaw clenched.

"I'm not done eating." Abel frowned.

"So, take it to-go, *duh*. We can finish eating at my house."

Abel looked at Pia with lowered eyes and then waved to get the attention of the waitress. She quickly returned with two to-go plates. Pia and Abel packed their food and bee-lined for the front door, walking a few yards in front of Zaya without any acknowledgements.

As they approached the car, Pia's stomach twisted. She felt drawn to the left side of the parking lot–and there they were. She turned to see Lilliana and Blaze staring as they walked toward her and Abel. [1]

The air thickened with unspoken tension. Lilliana's heart raced in her chest, her mind swirling with a mix of anger and anticipation. Blaze's stance was rigid, his eyes cold. Lilliana, though smaller, stood just as firm, her gaze burning into Pia.

"Look at little miss perfect," Lilliana drawled, as she stood ten feet away from with narrowed eyes. Pia's presence stirred something dark in Lilliana.

Pia sighed. "Not today. We're leaving."

Blaze smirked. "Oh, we definitely got unfinished business."

"Pia, get in the car," Abel said, his voice low, steady as he grabbed the passenger door handle.

---

1. **Book Soundtrack Cue**: "Run This Town" – Jay-Z, Rihanna, Kanye West.

But Lilliana wasn't done. A small pouch hung from her wrist, tucked beneath her bracelets. Inside, herbs, a poppet, and tokens charged with energy. She squeezed it, whispering under her breath, her heart pounding. She was going to humble her, remind her that not everything in her life could go as perfectly as it had been.

"Nah, nah, man. I got unfinished business with her. I don't know what the hell you did to me, but I'm not gon' let that shit slide," Blaze ranted.

Lilliana closed her eyes and began to whisper. She focused on Pia, tuning out Blaze's tirade. She placed her hand on the pouch, feeling the energy swell inside her, the whispers of her ancestors rising like an ancient tide.

"Dark spirits, make her stumble," Lilliana muttered under her breath, just loud enough for the words to form a connection. She imagined Pia falling to her knees, gasping for air. The thought brought a smirk to her lips.

"I don't know what your problem is, but this is a female! Not one of yo corner boys, so back the fuck up!" Abel told Blaze.

Lilliana continued, but when she opened her eyes, nothing happened. Pia was still standing by the car, all prim and proper, oblivious to the chaos she brought about in Lilliana. Lilliana frowned. She tried again, more forcefully this time. Her hand gripped the pouch tighter, her voice a harsh whisper.

"Let her trip, let her falter!"

"Nigga, fuck you! I got something for you, too," Blaze retorted.

Still, Pia remained untouched by Lilliana's silent rage. Lilliana's fingers began to tremble, the power she was trying to summon slipping away. The energy was there, swirling around her, but it refused to obey. Instead, a sudden coldness prickled the back of her neck. Something was *wrong*.

Pia looked at Lilliana. Pia's smile wavered for a moment, and for the first time, Lilliana saw something—something knowing, something dangerous—in her eyes. A small smirk ran across Pia's lips as if she knew exactly what Pia was trying to do. Then she looked past Lilliana, causing her to turn and look behind her.

"Lilliana, what the hell do you think you're doing?" Zaya hissed.

Lilliana froze immediately. She felt exposed, like a child caught in the act.

Zaya stood a few feet behind her, eyes wide, voice laced with betrayal.

"What?" Lilliana asked, suddenly breathless.

"That bag on your arm and *what* were you saying?" Zaya's voice grew louder.

Lilliana's breath hitched. She had failed, but worse than that, she had been seen.

"Zaya, this... it's nothing."

"Nah, I may not know exactly what that is, but I ain't no fool. You're out here, in public, trying to pull that *voodoo* nonsense on Pia?" Zaya asked, shockingly.

Lilliana's face flushed with a mix of shame and frustration. "You don't understand—she needs to be taken down a peg!"

Lilliana reached for Zaya's arm, but Zaya quickly pulled back.

"Don't *touch* me!" Zaya said. "I felt bad for you, but now I really feel sorry for you. You need to get help!" Zaya turned to look at Pia and mouthed *I'm sorry* before turning to walk away.

Blaze scoffed. "Man, forget her. Ain't none of these hoes your friends."

Lilliana swallowed hard as Zaya's Jeep sped away, taking the last sliver of her pride with it.

"Now, she drugged me or some shit and left me on the side of the road. You really thought I wasn't gonna handle that?" Blaze yelled.

The commotion was drawing attention now, onlookers peeking from inside the restaurant.

"You need to calm down before someone calls the police. And I didn't drug you," Pia told Blaze.

"Then explain how the hell I woke up on Highway 80 near the old mill. You and that white man did something to me." Blaze stepped closer, fists tightening.

Abel glanced at Pia, confusion and suspicion flickering across his face.

"What *happened* was you tried to kill us both, but you were so amped up that you slid and knocked yourself out. You could've woke up in jail, so you should be thanking me," Pia said.

Blaze let out a low, humorless chuckle. "Bitch, you expect me to believe that?"

"You the only bitch out here," Abel said.

Blaze began laughing menacingly. "Oh, pretty boy wanna play hero? I see you." Blaze's expression darkened. "Let's see how tough you really are."

He walked off, headed back to Lilliana's car.

"What you walking off for?" Abel taunted. "I'm right here."

Pia grabbed Abel's arm. "Let's go. Now."

"Nah, he's bluffing," Abel said, eyes locked on Blaze. "The nigga wanna be a bully and I can't stand a bully."

Then Lilliana snapped. Her face twisted with rage, tears spilling down her cheeks. "I lost Zaya because of *you*," she spat at Pia. "You poison everything!" Lilliana screamed. She was quickly losing control.

"You're delusional," Pia said. "Abel, *get in the car*."

Pia started the engine, but when she put the car in reverse, she couldn't move. Lilliana stood directly behind them, her body rigid, her stare unwavering.

"What is she doing?" Pia asked.

"I don't know. This shit has gotten crazy. What the hell has been going on, P. You've been leaving shit out," Abel said.

"I promise I'll tell you everything when we get back to my house. Just see if you can get her to move," Pia said.

"Damn, Lil, move out the way," Abel said after letting his window down.

Lilliana stood as if she had not heard Abel mutter a word.

Blaze exited the car and walked to Lilliana, looking her in the eyes.

"Lil, let us leave. Whatever is going on between you and Pia...we'll figure it out. Look at all these people looking at us," Abel said.

Lilliana broke her trance and looked around the parking lot. A small crowd grew and were watching them.

Lilliana took a step to the side, but turned back to focus her sight on Pia.

"Thank you," Abel whispered.

Blaze had stopped at his car but hadn't gotten in. Instead, his hand hovered near his waistband.

Pia's breath hitched. *No.*

Blaze turned, and in one fluid motion, he pulled the gun.

"Blaze, don't!" Pia shouted, jumping out of the car.

Pia looked in the rearview mirror and saw Blaze. She had an ill feeling in the pit of her stomach.

Lilliana grabbed her by the hair, yanking her back. Pia twisted, breaking free, and slammed Lilliana to the ground. She turned just in time to see Abel raise his hands, palms out.

"Blaze, you don't wanna do this," Abel said evenly.

With one swoop of her hand, Pia slammed Lilliana to the ground and jumped back.

Blaze grinned. "Oh, I *do*."

The world seemed to slow—

"Blaze, you wanna know the truth about that night?" Pia called, forcing his attention to her.

"I already know," Blaze growled.

Lilliana lunged at Pia.

A gunshot rang out.

Screams erupted. People ran in every direction.

And in the farthest corner of the parking lot, hidden in the shadows of a black Tahoe, Ms. Marie watched everything unfold.

CHAPTER FIFTEEN

P ia grabbed Lilliana fiercely. "I don't want to hurt you," Pia
said, her eyes flashing green unknowingly to her.

"Let's go!!" Lilliana yelled at Blaze in a grave tone. [1]

Pia ran over to Abel, horrified at the blood pouring on the ground.
There was a single gun-shot wound to his abdomen, but it did
major damage. Pia hovered over Abel. Her hands were slick with
Abel's blood, her breath ragged as she pressed down on his stomach, trying desperately to stop the bleeding. The world had narrowed down to this single moment—the gunshot, the horror in
Abel's eyes, and the unbearable reality of him slipping away. Panic
clawed at her, but deep beneath the surface, something powerful
stirred.

---

1. **Book Soundtrack Cue:** "Glory and Gore" – Lorde.

"Stay with me, Abel," she whispered, her voice trembling as she applied more pressure to the wound. The blood wouldn't stop. He groaned, his eyes fluttering open briefly, but his breaths were shallow, and his skin had turned ghostly pale.

Pia's heart thundered in her chest. She was running out of time.

Pia was afraid of using her powers in public, but no one was coming to help. In the back of her mind, Pia could hear Lilliana and Blaze's retreating footsteps, but she pushed the anger aside. Right now, all that mattered was Abel.

She closed her eyes, taking a shaky breath. *You can do this,* she told herself. *You have to do this!*

Her hands trembled as she hovered them over the wound, blood still seeping through her fingers. The surrounding air seemed to hum with energy, a soft vibration she could feel in her bones. She focused, reaching deep within herself, feeling the power unfurl like a blooming flower.

"Please," she whispered, her voice soft, almost pleading. "Let me save him."

A faint glow began to emanate from her palms, the energy gathering slowly, spreading over Abel's chest like golden tendrils of light. Pia's breath caught as she felt the power move through her, surging toward Abel's wound. Her hands grew warmer, and the glow intensified, pulsing with life.

Abel groaned again, his eyes flickering open, the pain in them slowly being replaced with something else—relief.

Pia knew she couldn't heal the wound completely. There would be too many questions that she couldn't answer, so she decided to heal it enough to make sure he wouldn't bleed out.

The blood flow slowed down, the wound knitting together beneath the soft, green light. Pia kept her hands steady, her focus unwavering as she directed the energy into him. She could feel his body responding, his breaths growing deeper, more stable. The color returned to his face, the deathly pallor fading away as life poured back into him.

"Pia...?" Abel's voice was weak but clear, his eyes wide as he looked up at her.

She smiled, tears filling her eyes as she let out a breath she hadn't realized she was holding. "I've got you," she whispered, her voice thick with emotion.

The glow faded, and the wound on Abel's chest now mostly healed.

Pia sat back, her hands still trembling, her heart pounding in her chest from the exertion. But she had done it—he was alive. She looked around the parking lot, and she was sure no one had seen her.

Abel blinked, his hand still gripping hers as he slowly sat up. His eyes were full of disbelief, confusion, but also gratitude. "How... how did you...?"

"Shhh" Pia said softly, as she heard sirens in the distance. "Shhh," she hushed him, forcing a shaky smile. "Help's coming."

"But...my wound," Abel said

"Is still there," Pia finished his statement. "Blaze shot you, but it's not life-threatening. You were going in and out. I'm glad you're more alert now."

Pia hated to lie, but she couldn't admit that she healed him. He was partly unconscious anyway, so she's going to have to stick to her story.

A police car skidded to a stop. Paramedics rushed in, pushing Pia aside as they took over. Abel's dazed gaze stayed on her, but she turned away, disappearing into the crowd before she had to answer for what she had done.

Later that night, Pia sat nervously in the dim candlelit parlor at the mansion. Her mind was a whirlwind of thoughts—Abel's face when she had healed him and Lilliana's vengeful gaze as she chanted her voodoo.

Ms. Marie sat across from Pia, her presence both calming and commanding. She was draped in a flowing, deep purple gown, her hair tied up in a high bun. Her dark eyes, always piercing and wise, settled on Pia with a knowing look.

She studied Pia from across the table, hands folded, expression unreadable. "No one saw you heal him?"

Pia swallowed hard, her hands twisting nervously in her lap. "I don't think so. He was half-conscious."

Ms. Marie exhaled, tapping a long nail against her chair's arm. "Your power is awakening faster than expected. You have to be careful."

"I *was* careful," Pia argued. "He was dying."

"Does he know?" Ms. Marie asked.

"He thinks he may have seen me do something to him, but I quickly dismissed what he was saying."

"So, he's suspicious," Ms. Marie sighed deeply.

Pia nodded, the gravity of the situation sinking in. "I know," she whispered. "But it's not just about me anymore. Lilliana and Blaze... they won't stop. And Lilliana—she's using voodoo."

THE LEGACY OF THE NURUS

At the mention of Lilliana's name, Ms. Marie's expression darkened. She leaned back in her chair; the candles flickered as if reacting to her sudden shift in energy. Ms. Marie's expression darkened. "Lilliana is lost. She's walking a dangerous path, and she's calling on forces she doesn't understand."

"She's dangerous," Pia said. "I saw it in her eyes. She's angry, and she blames me for everything—losing Zaya, losing control. She tried to use voodoo on me, and it failed, but it won't be the last time she tries."

"Lilliana's power comes from a place of pain and anger, and that makes her unpredictable. Voodoo is powerful, yes, but we are more powerful!"

Pia clenched her jaw. "I know she's hurting, but that doesn't justify what she's doing. We *all* go through things. I lost my mother and didn't turn to darkness."

Ms. Marie's gaze softened. "That's because you carry pain differently, baby. You've always been strong—too strong sometimes. But not everyone is built that way."

"What do I do...about Lilliana...and Blaze?" Pia asked.

Ms. Marie leaned forward, voice calm but firm. "Blaze is reckless. But Lilliana? She's more dangerous than you think. She blames you for everything, and people like that don't stop until they feel satisfied."

Pia's stomach twisted. "So what do I do?"

Ms. Marie's gaze held hers. "You prepare. And you decide—when the time comes, will you fight her? Or will you save her?"

A heavy silence filled the room before Ms. Marie changed the subject. "Any word from Raymond Windham?"

Pia shook her head. "Not since the night he saw me use my powers."

Ms. Marie's lips pursed. "Good. That man is watching you, Pia. And he isn't on our side."

Pia nodded. She didn't trust him either.

Ms. Marie reached across the table and squeezed Pia's hand. "You're not alone in this, baby. But things are changing fast. You need to be ready."

Pia swallowed hard. She wasn't sure what being "ready" even meant, but she knew one thing—this was far from over.

CHAPTER SIXTEEN

Pia awoke to the sound of silence—no phone buzzing or alerts pinging. She groaned, stretching before glancing at her screen.

She saw missed calls and texts from Nolan. It was 9 am, which meant her dad had already left for work. She hadn't heard a thing since she climbed into bed last night. As she tapped her phone screen for what felt like the hundredth time, her frustration grew with each passing second. She let out a sigh, glancing at the empty Wi-Fi bars at the top of her phone. [1]

"Come on...not today," she muttered to herself, swiping down to refresh again.

---

1. **Book Soundtrack Cue**: "Radioactive" – Imagine Dragons.

NIE HARVEY

With a resigned groan, she moved over to her laptop, hoping to send a message through Connexta. But as soon as she clicked the browser, the same error message appeared: No Internet Connection.

She glanced toward the modem sitting in the corner of the living room, the usual cluster of blinking lights looking unusually still.

No lights.

Pia frowned and moved quickly over to the modem, crouching down to inspect it. She clicked the power button, unplugged it, waited, then plugged it back in—nothing. Not a single flicker of life.

"Okay," she whispered, standing up and rubbing her forehead. She grabbed her phone again, ready to call Abel, but then realized that without Wi-Fi, even making a call was useless with little mobile data. Her signal was barely hanging on, flickering between one bar and none.

Deciding to check outside, Pia slipped on her house shoes and walked out the front door. She looked over at Abel's house and wished he were home. Yesterday seemed like a distant nightmare. A slight breeze tugged at the rosebush on her front lawn. She noticed a few neighbors standing outside their houses, phones in hand, glancing around with the same confused expressions she had. The subtle unease in the air was unmistakable.

"Hey, do y'all have internet?" Pia called out to the Sudduth's standing near their car, scrolling furiously on their phones.

Mrs. Sudduth shook her head, looking frustrated. "Nope. Ours went down about an hour ago. Phones too."

Pia's stomach twisted. *Phones too?*

"I can't even get through to the news app," Mr. Sudduth added, tapping his screen. "Ain't never seen anything like this."

Pia felt a strange twinge of concern creep up her spine. "Same here. I thought it was just me, but..." Pia thought back to Abel's rant about the latest conspiracy theory.

Mrs. Sudduth nodded. "I've already seen a few people driving out to check other parts of town. Some said it's down over by the River Market too. It's like the whole network just collapsed. I hate I got rid of my landline."

A sinking feeling settled in Pia's chest. Windsorville wasn't exactly a tech hub, but a total blackout? That didn't just *happen.*

"Let me check on Abel," she murmured, heading back inside.

As she moved through the house, she thought about the past 24 hours—Blaze pulling a gun, Abel bleeding out, Lilliana trying to hex her. And now, the whole town was offline like someone had flipped a switch.

A knock at the door startled her.

"Pia!"

Pia turned to see Zaya walking into the house, phone in hand, and a worried expression on her face. She grabbed Pia in a warm embrace, tears stinging the corners of her eyes.

"Pia, I'm sorry. I swear I had no idea that Lilliana was using voodoo!! You know I wouldn't be okay with that!" Zaya said.

Pia sighed, relieved that Zaya saw the real Lilliana.

"I know," Pia said. "I'm glad you came by."

"Me too. Then, I heard Abel got shot and now something crazy is going on with the internet," Zaya rambled on.

"Abel's at the Windsorville Medical. I'm actually about to head up there to see him."

"I tried to call him this morning, but my service sucks!"

"Have you heard anything about the internet?"

"Girl, the internet's out everywhere." Zaya let out a frustrated sigh. "I can't even get through to anyone. No updates, no alerts. It's like we're cut off."

The weight of the situation began to settle on Pia. The entire town was suddenly isolated, disconnected from the rest of the world. In a digital age where everything relied on constant connectivity, being plunged into this kind of silence felt jarring, almost surreal.

"We need to figure out what's going on," Pia said, glancing around. "If this is widespread, it could be bigger than we think. Maybe some kind of massive outage, or... I don't know," Pia said, sounding defeated.

Zaya nodded, her brows furrowing. "You're still in your clothes from yesterday. Go get dressed, so we can go check on Abel. I'll drive."

As Pia and Zaya drove toward the center of town, the normally busy streets were oddly subdued. Businesses had their doors open, but many of the storefronts that relied on online systems for transactions were now either closed or dealing with long lines of confused customers. A small crowd had gathered outside the coffee shop, their conversations filled with worried murmurs.

They pulled into the hospital parking lot. Pia scrolled to her messages to see what room Abel texted her last night: 405.

"I know you hate hospitals, P. We don't have to stay long."

"Thanks, but I'm okay. Abel probably don't know what to do with himself without Connexta," she chuckled.

The hospital was eerily quiet. The electronic check-in screens were blank, idle with no data streaming in. Phones, normally buzzing with notifications, lie dormant on desks or in pockets. There's no Wi-Fi to connect to, no cellular data. The outage has plunged the hospital into an eerie stillness. A nurse moved quickly through the hallway, her face pinched with concern. She held a clipboard instead of a tablet, jotting notes by hand. Behind her, a doctor spoke quietly to a colleague, frustration seeping into his voice as they discussed the difficulty of accessing patient records without the internet. Paper charts and handwritten logs are scattered across their workstation, a chaotic throwback to an era long past.

"Even the hospital's down," Zaya murmured.

Pia pressed the elevator button, but nothing happened. A hand-written sign was taped beside it: *Out of Order.*

"Stairs it is," Pia sighed.

When they reached Abel's room, Pia pushed the door open to find him propped up in bed, cracking jokes with a nurse. He grinned as soon as he saw them. The sterile scent of antiseptic and the soft hum of fluorescent lights filled Abel's room. There was a flickering TV mounted high on the wall, displaying nothing but static. Abel was lying in the hospital bed on top of crisp white sheets. A thick bandage was wrapped around his abdomen where the bullet struck, the dried blood staining the gauze at the edges.

"Hey, iron man," Zaya said as she walked in the room with a big grin.

Abel looked up, eyes lit with joy to see Zaya and Pia together.

"The gang is back!" he announced, wincing slightly as he shifted.

"Take is easy," Pia warned, hopping on the edge of his bed.

Zaya folded her arms. "How are you smiling after getting shot?"

Abel smirked. "I'm built different."

Pia chuckled, but her eyes flicked to the bandage on his side. *He shouldn't be healing this fast.*

"The doctor said my wound's closing up quicker than expected," Abel said, reading her expression. "I told him I must be a mutant."

Zaya rolled her eyes. "Boy, please."

Pia forced a small smile, but inside, she was panicking. Had she healed him too much? Would the doctors start asking questions?

"I hate that happened to you," Zaya continued.

"Yeah, me too," Pia said.

"I gave the police my statement, and they've been coming up here to keep me updated. Blaze was picked up this morning."

"Good, they should've picked up looney toons too," Pia said.

"Where are your parents, Abel? Have they already been here?"

"No, and I don't want them here, either," Abel responded bluntly.

After a few seconds of awkward silence, Abel said, "This internet thing is weird, too, right?"

"Whatever, Abel. We don't know what's going on. Your conspiracy is still just a conspiracy."

"So, what have you been doing? You can't get on your phone or watch tv. That sucks," Zaya said.

"Let's just say I've been keeping busy. Bianca just left," Abel said slyly.

"Oh, lord. You just won't stop, will you?" Pia said.

"Not until one of those girls bop you in the head," Zaya said, as she playfully hit Abel with a pillow.

A curvy woman with caramel skin and waist-length braids stormed in, her heels clicking against the tile. She had a mix of fear and frustration etched on her face. Dressed in tight jeans and a low-cut blouse, her heavy heels echo against the linoleum floor. She had heard about Abel's injury through a mutual friend.

"Oh my God, Abel!" she gasps, rushing to his side and grabbing his hand. "Why didn't anyone tell me sooner?"

Abel groaned. "Damn. Hey, Shay."

Shay whipped her head around, her eyes narrowing. "Who are they?"

"His *friends*," Pia said flatly.

"His *girlfriend*," Shay added.

Zaya let out a low whistle. "Oh, this just got good."

Before Pia could respond, a nurse entered with a bouquet of flowers and *Get Well Soon* balloons. She set them down next to the other gifts Abel had already received.

"Damn, player," Zaya teased. "Who sent all these?"

Shay's eyes narrowed. "Yeah, Abel. Who?"

Pia smirked. "Welp. That's our cue. It's a bit too crowded in here. How about we go and get you something other than hospital food?"

"Yeah, and make sure it's not crowded when we get back," Zaya snapped.

Abel's eyes pleaded for help, but he knew he was left to deal with Shay on his own.

The girls headed to one of Abel's favorite spots, Al's Smash Burgers. They noticed there weren't many cars out, but they did see a few armored cars with soldiers driving around. The sight was uncanny. For the first time, the quiet of the town felt oppressive, like an invisible barrier had been placed over them all. Pia couldn't shake the feeling that whatever had caused this wasn't just a random glitch. Something was wrong, and now they were cut off, left to figure it out on their own.

"Sheesh, let's turn the radio on. It's too quiet for my liking," Zaya said as she scanned different stations to get to her favorite hip hop channel.

"Wait, go back," Pia said. "Let me see something."

Pia leaned forward, twisting the knob to tune in more clearly. The voice of a government official came through, stiff and cold, making her heart race.

"... the blackout, we understand, has already caused significant disruption to daily life within the first six hours. However, it was a necessary measure due to an imminent national threat. For the safety of our citizens, we had no choice but to disable communication networks and all electronic infrastructure. This decision was not made lightly..."

Pia's breath caught in her throat. "Imminent threat?" she muttered, her fingers tightening around the radio dial. She turned up the volume, listening intently as the broadcast continued.

"Though details of the threat remain classified for national security reasons, we assure the public that these measures were taken to prevent widespread harm. We ask for your patience and cooperation as our forces work to neutralize the danger."

"What the hell is really going on?" Zaya asked.

The official's voice droned on, but Pia's mind was spinning. What kind of threat could justify shutting down the entire grid? A threat big enough to plunge millions into darkness—yet they couldn't even tell people what it was?

"I don't know," Pia responded as if she was in a trance, "but I need to go see my dad and I want to check on Ms. Marie."

"Ok, well, let's grab Abel's food first. Then, we can swing by your house so you can get your car. I'll take Abel his food and you go do what you need to do."

The static of silence filled the air as they continued down the road, their eyes scanning the town.

"It seems like most people are home today," Zaya said.

"Right, and did you see the Starbucks and Chick-fil-A lines–empty?! This is so *weird*," Pia responded.

They pulled into the drive-thru lane of Al's. As they rolled down the window, the speaker crackled with static.

"Welcome to Big Burger. Uh, sorry, folks, our system's down—no internet," came a voice, sounding slightly frazzled. "You'll have to, uh, pay with cash if you're ordering."

Zaya glanced at Pia with raised eyebrows. "Cash? Do we even have any?"

Pia rummaged through her purse, producing a crumpled twenty-dollar bill and a handful of coins. "Looks like we're about to find out," she said with a smirk.

They pulled up to the speaker, and Zaya leaned out the window. "We're ready to order."

The voice on the other end sighed, clearly improvising. "Okay, we're just writing everything down by hand. What can I get you?"

"Let me get a Smash burger with cheese, a fry, and, uh, do you still have milkshakes?"

The line went quiet for a second before the worker responded. "Shakes are down too, sorry. No internet for the machines."

Pia leaned closer, looking at the menu. "Let me get a coke."

"Got it. Pull around."

As they rolled up to the window, the usual bustle of a fast-food joint felt strangely muted. The employees inside weren't huddled over screens or punching in orders on digital registers. Instead, one girl was scribbling on a notepad, while another handed out a brown paper bag to the car ahead. The air smelled like sizzling burgers and frying oil, but there was a distinct lack of beeps and buzzes from behind the counter.

Zaya handed over the crumpled twenty, and the girl at the window paused for a moment, calculating the total in her head, then scribbling on a piece of paper. "That'll be...$15.75."

Pia and Zaya watched her fumble through a little plastic container of coins to make change. The whole process felt slower, but also a little more human. No digital transactions, no automated voices—just people trying to keep things moving.

"Here you go!" The girl handed them their change and passed over the bag of food. "Sorry about the wait."

"Thanks," Zaya said, smiling. "Good luck in there."

As the two entered Pia's neighborhood, they saw more people outside. For a moment, Pia and Zaya simply watched, reminded of how simple and joyful life could be without the constant buzz of technology. It was like the whole town had taken a collective pause, and in that pause, life became a little more vibrant, a little more real. Yet Pia still couldn't shake the eerie feeling she had in the pit of her stomach.

"Okay, girl, I'll head back to the hospital once I finish making my rounds. If you need me, send a pigeon," Pia chuckled as she hopped out of Zaya's jeep.

"Right, I keep carrier pigeons for situations like this," Zaya said sarcastically.

Pia quickly hopped in her car and headed to the mechanic shop. She pulled in and noticed that there weren't many cars there today.

"Hey, sweet pea," Pierre said as he walked out to her car. "I was wondering when you would show up," Pierre grinned.

Pia got out of the car and gave her dad a hug. "Dad, this is crazy, right? Was the internet working when you left home?"

"I didn't notice until I got here. Come in and have a seat."

Pia stood in the doorway of the mechanic shop, the familiar scent of motor oil and grease hanging in the air. The usual hum of machinery was absent, replaced by the soft clinking of metal tools and the muffled sounds of the radio—a static-filled station that seemed to be struggling without the internet.

"How is it going here at the shop?" Pia asked.

"It's barely going. It's been a day of old-school mechanics. No digital diagnostics, no emails from parts suppliers. Feels like we've gone back in time."

"How's that going?" Pia asked, curious.

"It's been a mix. Slower, for sure. We can't run the diagnostics like we usually do, so I've had to rely on my ears and hands. You know, just like the old days. At first, it felt kind of frustrating, but... now, I'm starting to remember how much I actually know about cars without all the gadgets."

"So, you're saying it's not all bad?" Pia grinned.

"Depends on the day. When the internet first went out, we were in a panic—couldn't order parts, couldn't access customer records, nothing. Had to call suppliers on the phone, if you can believe that," he said with a grin. "Turns out some of these guys don't even know how to handle orders without their systems. But now? We've adjusted. Customers have had to slow down, too. No instant quotes or 'let me Google what's wrong.' We've been explaining things face-to-face again."

"Any news of when the internet will be back up?"

"No, I don't know anything right now."

"Got it. Well, I just wanted to check on you since I couldn't text or call."

"Let me give you the shop number."

Pierre went over to the counter, got a pen and notepad, and wrote the phone number down. "If you're near a landline or your cell phone has any data, you can always call the shop. When I leave here, I'll be headed straight home."

"Thanks, dad. I'm going to go check on Ms. Marie next. Then I'll swing by the hospital to see Abel and I'll be home shortly after that."

Pia stood up and Pierre gave her a gentle kiss on the forehead. "Be careful and I'll see you tonight."

CHAPTER
SEVENTEEN

T he usual hum of Windsorville had fallen into an uneasy quiet after two weeks without the internet. Even with people
chatting at the coffee shops, kids playing in the street, and friends
gathering at events, there was an uncertainty and uneasiness that
hung in the air. Ms. Marie found herself jotting down supply lists
manually, often relying on memory and phone calls with suppliers,
while Pia had an influx of girls whose parents replaced screen time
with dance shoes. Online classes for college students were switched
to in-person. Windsorville had gone back three decades, and no
one understood why.

Pia sat on the couch in her yoga pants and t-shirt, trying to decide
which board game to pull from underneath the coffee table. It was
Friday, and she looked forward to the newly founded game night
with Abel and Zaya. Pierre walked into the living room and Pia
watched her dad as he finished tying his tie.

"How do I look?" Pierre asked, brushing off invisible dust from his blazer. "Not bad, huh?"

Pia forced a small smile, hoping her distaste for Lilliana wouldn't leak into her expression. "You look good, Dad. Like, *date good*," she laughed, hoping it would cover the tension brewing beneath her words.

"Thanks, sweet pea," he said, his voice warm. "Enjoy game night. I called in a pizza for you all to enjoy."

"Aww, thanks dad," Pia responded. "Have fun."

As Pierre grabbed his keys, Pia worried about what would happen if things got serious between him and Ms. Jiménez. Maybe she'd let it slide this time, keep her opinions about Lilliana to herself... for now. But if she had to deal with Lilliana on a regular basis, well, that was a battle she wasn't prepared to back down from.

As Pierre opened the front door, Abel stumbled in.

"I was just about to knock," he said with a broad smile.

"Abel, you know lately it seems like you live here. I see you almost every day," Pierre commented.

"I agree. I think it would be better if I moved in."

"Yeah...right," Pierre said sarcastically as he stepped outside and closed the door.

"When's Zaya getting here?" Abel asked, pulling Monopoly onto the table.

"Oh, no! We played that last week."

"So what?"

"So...you cheat! That's what."

"Okay, you can be the bank this time."

"It doesn't matter. You'll still find a way to cheat. Zaya said she was running late, but she'll be here soon."

"Okay, cool. I want to talk to you about something Pia, but you have to be opened minded."

"I want to talk to you, too...and you have to be opened minded."

"You go first," Abel insisted.

"Well..." Pia said blushing, "I have been seeing someone."

"Whhhaattt??" Abel said, shocked.

"Who?!"

"Calm down! It's ol boy from the club that night, Nolan."

"So...when you say talking...y'all been hooking up?" Abel asked, holding his breath.

"No, I mean just what I said...TALKING. We haven't went on an official date, but we are going out tomorrow night. I just wanted you to know."

"You really like this dude, Pia?"

"Yes, Abel. I do. He's sweet, thoughtful, caring, considerate. I really, really like him."

"Aight, P. Don't get him messed up."

"Oh, let me guess. You been shot now, so you're tough?" Pia giggled.

"Call it what you want, but he better treat ya right. Where y'all going tomorrow?"

"La Mariso," Pia smiled.

"What time?"

"Damn, inspector gadget."

"It's not like you can just drop your location right now. I need all the details, P."

"See, I knew you were going to act like this."

"Like what? I'm just looking out for you."

"I hear you. I'll give you the details, but don't piss me off and don't bring your ass up there."

"I can't promise you nothing. I like to eat, too."

"Whatever, boy. What is it that you wanted to tell me?"

"I find out some more information about this internet blackout thing."

"Go on," Pia said.

"There's a group of people called the *Nurus*."

"The *what*?" Pia echoed, brows furrowing and eyes widening.

Abel's expression grew intense, his voice barely a whisper now. "The Nurus. They're, like, these...supernatural people who live among us. Not like ghosts or anything, but... enhanced. Some say they've been around for centuries, blending in. And supposedly, the government is terrified of them."

Pia froze, wondering where this was headed.

"Think about it," he insisted, his eyes gleaming. "What if the government's afraid the Nurus could, like, overpower us? So they killed the internet to cut off their communications-isolating them from each other. Without it, they're just as blind as we are."

Pia tilted her head, watching him with a mix of amusement and intrigue. "So, you're saying the government just...flipped a switch? To go after a bunch of so-called superhumans?" she said nervously.

Abel nodded solemnly. "And there's more. People say that this is just the beginning. That the Nurus have been preparing for a long time, and this internet blackout?"

"Wait, Abel. Where are you getting this information?"

"A few of us who live here and were in the Connexta groups meet up once a week to share information about what's going on."

"How do you know if any of this is true?"

"I don't, but they haven't missed so far? But Pia, isn't that crazy?! Supernatural people living among us."

"Yeah, bananas," Pia said dryly.

"It's not that. It's just a lot to process," Abel said.

The two jumped as they heard a hard knock on the door.

Abel jumped up and walked quickly to the window, where he saw Zaya's car.

"Why are you beating the door down?" Abel asked Zaya, who rushed into the living room.

"Y'all not gon' believe this shit," Zaya said huffing, trying to catch her breath.

"Breathe, Za. Come and have a seat," Pia said.

"What's going on?"

"Blaze."

Abel immediately became flustered at the mention of his name. His eyes darkened and lips tightened.

"Fuck that nigga. I don't want to hear about him."

"Well, he's out of jail and he's been robbing places left and right. He just hit Linda's Jewelry downtown."

"A lot of the cameras need Wi-Fi to work, so how do you know it was him?"

"Well, for one, he's been bragging about his feats since he got out. On top of that, it's not just him. It's his whole crew, so word of mouth is traveling fast cause you know people can't keep shit to themselves. Then, someone saw Lilliana's car leaving the jewelry store!!" Zaya said excitedly.

Pia's stomach twisted. Blaze back in the streets was one thing. But Lilliana? Involved?

"This is a problem that needs to be handled," Abel said, gritting his teeth.

"It won't be too long before the police catch up with him again."

"I'm worried it may get out of hand before they do. He's taking advantage of this internet situation and that shit ain't right."

Pia felt overwhelmed. Hearing Abel talk about Nurus and Zaya talk about Blaze was too much to deal with at the moment.

Pia looked at Abel. His body was tense, and his face showed anger in every crevice. Zaya looked genuinely worried, which is not her style at all. Pia felt compelled to find a solution, but she didn't want to risk exposure...again.

Knock. Knock.

Pia awoke to knocks on her bedroom door. She, Abel, and Zaya had stayed up until 2 am playing Trivial Pursuit, Monopoly, and Jenga. She rolled over to look at the time: 10:12 a.m.

"Come in," Pia said groggily.

"Hey, sweet pea, I was hoping you would come to the town hall meeting with me at 12," Pierre said.

Pia sat up in her bed. "What town hall meeting? Why is there a town hall meeting today?"

"Well, I got up this morning and went to the grocery store to grab a few things. I noticed a cluster of flyers plastered around town for a town hall meeting. People are starting to get antsy around here."

"What do you think the meeting is about, dad?" Pia asked.

"You know, everyone has been feeling the effects of the blackout, with no easy access to information—or each other. But the bigger issue is the recent uptick in rumors of break-ins, robberies, and a general sense of unease with these gang members."

"Yeah, I heard about that, too. I'll go with you."

"I also saw a few police cars riding around reeaalll slow with their lights off and just behind them, there was a military vehicle. I'm trying to make sense of it all, but I can't," Pierre said with furrowed brows.

"I've been seeing military trucks at the mason lodge across from my studio...but they were here before the blackout," Pia realized.

"Yeah, something's not right, baby girl. In times like this, our town needs to stick together. Hopefully, we can find a better way than to steal from each other."

"Right."

"You have time to eat breakfast before we leave. I got your favorite cereal," Pierre chuckled.

Pia jumped in the shower and got dressed. She couldn't help but question their new reality. As she cut up bananas for her cereal, she was reminded of her date with Nolan.

"Oh, dad," Pia said with a grin.

"Yeah?"

"I forgot to mention I have a date tonight."

Pierre snapped his head in Pia's direction, appearing amused, confused, and shocked. "With who?!" Pierre said.

"His name is Nolan. He's a real estate agent. We're going to La Mariso at 6. I'll be home by 9," Pia said quickly.

"Mhm, hmm, so where did you meet Nolan?" Pierre inquired.

"We met at a nightclub. I know. I know. He's super sweet, and he's been the perfect gentlemen."

"Well, I can't wait to meet this Nolan guy."

"Me too," Pia said with a smirk. "I'm almost ready. We can head out in 15 minutes."

The father-daughter duo pulled up to city hall and noticed an overflowing parking lot and street. Many people must have gotten word of the meeting. They found a park at the flower shop across the street and proceeded to the town hall meeting room. City hall was packed to the brim, a sea of tense faces filling every seat, spilling into aisles and leaning against the walls.[1]

Pia and Pierre sat near the back, watched the mayor, a small, silver-haired woman named Leslie Jenkins, tap her microphone, signaling for order. The room quieted, though tension hung thick in the air. Pia rubbed her eyes, seeing a few green spots among the crowd. Maybe she was just tired.

"Thank you all for being here," she began, her voice firm but weary. "Since the internet blackout, we've seen a sharp increase in incidents around town: break-ins, vandalism, and in some cases, gang violence. I know you're all concerned, and that's why we're here—to discuss solutions and next steps."

A hand shot up from the front. It was Greg, a local store owner. His face was red, his jaw set.

"People are getting desperate, Mayor! My shop was broken into twice this week! We need more than just 'discussions'—where are the officers when we need them?"

Murmurs rippled through the crowd, and Pierre caught snippets of other complaints: missing tools, late-night intruders, cars stolen from driveways.

---

1. **Book Soundtrack Cue**: "Drop the World" – Lil Wayne ft. Eminem.

Sheriff Collins, sitting beside the mayor, cleared his throat and leaned forward. "I understand your frustration, Greg," he said, his voice carrying a gravelly authority. "We're stretched thin. Communications are down, and without the internet, we're struggling to coordinate effectively. We've increased foot patrols and luckily, we have a bit of military presence around town. But resources are limited."

A woman in the back row stood up. "So, we're supposed to just fend for ourselves?" she asked, a note of panic in her voice. "The blackout could go on for who knows how long. Security cameras don't work. I don't even feel safe walking to my car at night!"

Pia felt the crowd's fear swell, feeding on itself, voices overlapping in urgent whispers and shouts. It was as if the internet's disappearance had taken with it a certain sense of safety, of reassurance.

Mayor Jenkins raised her hands, calling for calm. "Please, everyone! We're not going to let our community fall apart. There's already a team working to establish a watch schedule, so we can cover each neighborhood without putting too much strain on any one household."

"Neighborhood watch?" A young man scoffed. "So now *we're* the police?"

The sheriff's gaze grew steely. "Yes, son, you are. For the time being, we're all going to have to look out for each other. If you see something suspicious, report it to the nearest officer or town official. We need to stand together."

A deep silence followed. Pia could feel the weight of the sheriff's words sinking in. The sense of neighborly trust had been replaced by a new understanding of survival.

The mayor glanced at the clock, taking a deep breath. "Thank you for your input. We'll be assigning neighborhood captains by tomorrow. Let's keep our families safe, keep each other safe."

As the meeting dispersed, Pia saw Blaze standing by the door. A few people noticed him as well, their voices low with whispers and faces taut with worry. Whatever came next, they'd be facing it together—but Pia could feel the silent question hanging in the air: *For how long?*

CHAPTER EIGHTEEN

The dim glow of candles flickered across the cozy little restaurant as Pia sat across from Nolan, feeling her cheeks flush every time he flashed that easy smile. She had almost forgotten just how handsome he was. He was older and had that polished charm, but something about him felt different, softer, more genuine than she'd expected. [1]

"So," he said, his voice smooth as he leaned in a little closer, "How has dance being going?"

"Great!" Pia smiled. "It's... kind of like my second home."

He took a sip of his drink, watching her over the rim. "Real estate isn't *quite* as rewarding as teaching kids to dance, I'm sure."

---

1. **Book Soundtrack Cue**: "Pretty Little Birds" – SZA ft. Isaiah Rashad.

"Oh, come on," she laughed. "People love real estate! You're helping people find homes, build businesses... I'd say that's pretty meaningful."

"Maybe, but things have been a little odd lately. With the internet down, deals are taking longer to close, and people are uneasy. It's almost like everything's moving through molasses."

Pia nodded, feeling the weight of the past couple of weeks. "It's like time slowed down, isn't it? I haven't had to work without the internet... maybe ever. It's forcing us all to talk more, though," she added. "Even my students! Instead of scrolling through their phones before class, they're actually... connecting."

"Yeah, it's strange," he said, glancing out the window as if considering something carefully. He took a breath, his expression shifting slightly, growing more serious. "And it's not just the outage. I mean, remember I told you about the Masonic Lodge?"

"Yeah, I remember," Pia said.

"Something's been off, especially with the new leadership."

"The lodge?" Pia asked, intrigued.

The two were interrupted by the waitress, who put out their entrees and took up their salad plates. They ordered the same dish: a cut of tenderloin, perfectly seared and topped with a dab of herb-infused butter. Beside it, truffle mashed potatoes with a subtle earthiness that paired beautifully with the steak accompanied by grilled asparagus spears lightly drizzled with balsamic to add a hint of sweetness. Nolan nodded at the waitress as a thank you.

"Yeah," he said, lowering his voice slightly. "I've been part of it for a while. It used to feel like a place where we'd come together to help the community, you know? But lately, some of the guys who've taken over, they're... different. I have this feeling, like they're after something more than tradition and charity work. I actually heard a few of the guys talking and one said, 'we're closer than we've ever been to capture.' Whatever that means," Nolan shrugged.

She shivered slightly, noticing the way his face had grown tense. "Do you think it's connected to the internet outage?"

He tilted his head, meeting her gaze with an intensity that made her pulse quicken. "I don't know. But something tells me there's more going on than they're letting on."

Pia bit her lip, feeling the spark of curiosity light up within her. She wanted to press him, to find out more, but his face softened, and he reached out, his hand resting gently on hers.

"But," he said with a smile that sent a shiver down her spine, "I'd rather talk about you. Tell me more about your studio, Pia. I think I could listen to you talk about dance all night."

She laughed, feeling herself melt under his gaze. "You're definitely a charmer."

"You make it easy," Nolan grinned, flashing his perfect whites. "Do you think your dad likes me?"

"He tries to play tough, but I'm sure he does," Pia said as she slid her entrée closer to her. "This looks amazing."

Pia took a bite of her asparagus and reached for her glass of water. The water was rippling, tiny waves spinning inside the glass, though her hand had barely touched it. Then, almost as if responding to her touch, the water lifted—just a fraction, just enough to make her heart race. She pulled her hand back, hoping Nolan hadn't noticed, but he was busy taking a sip of his own drink.

Pia squeezed her hand into a fist under the table, trying to calm her racing thoughts. But when she glanced down at her hand, her breath caught in her throat. A soft, golden glow pulsed from her palm, radiating warmth in a way that felt both comforting and terrifying.

"Pia? Are you okay?"

Nolan's voice sounded far away as her mind spun with questions. Her fingers tingled, and she clenched them tightly, willing the glow to fade. She couldn't risk an accidental display here, not in public, not in front of Nolan.

What's happening to me now? Am I losing control? Or is this something else? I gotta get out of here!

Pia forced a smile, gathering her purse from her lap and standing abruptly. "I'm sorry, Nolan. I feel a bit nauseous. Can we pick back up some other time?"

"Oh... yeah, sure," he said, his brow furrowed with confusion, but he didn't press further. He signaled the waiter to bring the check.

"I'll wait outside. I just need some fresh air," she said.

Before he could say anything else, she turned and hurried toward the door, her hand still tingling with that strange golden warmth.

Nolan's car pulled up in front of Pia's house, its engine humming softly in the quiet night. Pia unclasped her seatbelt, offering a quick smile, though her thoughts were still buzzing.

"Thanks for tonight," she said. "I had a great time."

"Yeah, me too," Nolan replied, smiling back with a softness that made her heart ache. He seemed so genuine, so complete in the moment, while she was already halfway out of it. She hated ending things abruptly earlier, but the glow in her hand had shaken her.

As she reached for the door handle, Nolan stopped her with a gentle touch on her shoulder. "Hey, is everything okay?" His face softened with concern. "Did I do something wrong?"

"No, no," she said, brushing it off with a light laugh that felt forced even to her. "It's just... I think I'm coming down with something.

Nothing to worry about." She tried to inject a bit of cheer into her tone, hoping he'd buy it.

Nolan studied her face, his eyes tracing her expression with quiet intensity. Finally, he nodded, though she could tell he wasn't fully convinced. "Well, let me know if you need anything."

With one last look, she pushed open the door and stepped out, breathing in the cool night air. She waved as he pulled away, watching his taillights disappear down the street before turning toward her car. Her hand was normal now, just her own fingers in the dim streetlight, but the memory of the warmth lingered.

She slipped into her car. Steeling herself, she murmured under her breath, "Whatever this is, I need to figure it out. Before it gets out of control." As she started the car, she hoped her dad didn't hear, and she began to quickly back out of the driveway.

Pia knocked on Ms. Marie's door, the familiar scent of sage and lavender drifting through the small gap as it opened. Ms. Marie stood there in her flowing wrap, her eyes sharp and curious, as if she could sense Pia's tension even before a word was spoken.

"Come in, come in," Ms. Marie said, ushering Pia inside. "I was just making tea. Would you like a cup?"

"Sure," Pia responded. "Where's Tay?"

Marie chuckled at the thought of Tay. "Tay had an eventful day. We swam, walked in the park, and worked in the garden. My sweet boy is tired and gone to bed."

Pia followed her to the cream and rose-colored kitchen, settling into the cushioned chair by the table as Ms. Marie poured a cup of tea and slid it across to her. "What's weighing on you, child?"

Pia took a breath, glancing down at her hands. "Something... weird happened to me tonight," she began, her voice soft. "I wasn't even trying to use my power, but I accidentally...I think I made water move. It was just in a glass on the table, but when I touched it, the water started swirling, like it was responding to me." She shook her head, still not quite believing it herself.

Ms. Marie's eyebrows lifted slightly, and she gave a thoughtful nod. "And how did that make you feel?" she asked carefully.

Pia stared down at her hands, frowning. "Confused. And that's not even the weirdest part," she said, glancing up. "Usually, when I use my power, my hands glow green, you know that. But tonight... they glowed gold. I don't understand what that means."

Ms. Marie's heart skipped a beat, but she forced herself to remain calm, taking a slow sip of her tea to hide the smile tugging at her lips. Gold. The color that only a rare few ever saw—

"Where were you?" Ms. Marie inquired.

"I was having dinner with a friend, and before you ask, nobody saw it," Pia assured.

"You're certain it was gold?" Ms. Marie asked, feigning a slight frown as she leaned closer, as if contemplating the significance. "Not a trick of the candlelight?"

"No," Pia replied firmly. "I know what I saw. It felt different, too… warmer. Like it was more than just light." She looked at Ms. Marie, searching her face. "Do you think it could mean something?"

"Well," Ms. Marie said, choosing her words carefully, "it's rare, but as your powers grow, you may start experiencing… shifts, signs that your abilities are evolving. And the color of your aura can change based on your connection to certain energies."

"But I didn't ask for more power—I can barely control the power I already have." Her voice grew softer. "I'm not sure I'm ready for more."

Ms. Marie reached out and covered Pia's hand with her own, her voice gentle but steady. "Pia, powers are like rivers. You can't always control where they flow, but you can learn to trust the current. Whatever's happening, you're meant to handle it."

Ms. Marie gave Pia's hand a reassuring squeeze. "Just take it as it comes, and know that whatever is meant for you, you'll be ready when the time comes." She kept her true thoughts close. But for now, she would let Pia take this journey one step at a time.

Raymond sat alone in his office, the muted hum of the lodge settling into silence as the last of the evening's members departed. His fingers tapped a steady rhythm against the polished mahogany desk, his mind torn between loyalty to his duty and an unfamiliar sense of indebtedness.

He leaned back in his leather chair, eyes narrowing as he stared at the framed certificates and symbols adorning the walls, each a reminder of the order's values—truth, duty, protection. Reporting Pia would be the responsible thing to do, he told himself, the right thing. She'd exhibited powers beyond what they could monitor safely, powers that were rare and unpredictable.

And yet, he couldn't shake the image of that night. If it hadn't been for her intervention, he wouldn't be sitting here now, wrestling with this decision.

Raymond ran a hand over his jaw, lost in thought. If he brought her in, there would be protocols, tests, analyses. But he knew too well what those tests involved, the invasive questioning, the scrutiny, the way each power was probed until it broke or revealed its secrets. Pia didn't deserve that. Not after she'd saved him.

But if he left her alone, who knew what powers might awaken in her? If she continued to develop unchecked, the risks could be devastating—for her and everyone around her. He sighed, conflicted.

An idea formed, quiet but insistent, the beginnings of a compromise that might solve his dilemma. Raymond felt a twinge of guilt, but he forced it aside. It wasn't manipulation; he told himself. It was caution. An invitation. He could bring Pia in under a gentler pretense. A simple interview, he'd call it. A government interview to understand the impact of no internet. It wouldn't be suspicious; in fact, it would make her feel like part of the government's work, not its target. Once she agreed, he could arrange for subtle tests, assessments she wouldn't even realize were happening. He wondered, though, if the tests *could* break her.

Picking up his pen, he began to jot down notes, crafting his plan with careful precision. He would need to sound genuine, friendly, and Pia would need to feel like this was an opportunity, not an obligation.

He looked out his window and saw Pia's car parked outside the studio. He walked over and began rehearsing the words over and over until he made it to the studio door. Knocking quickly, he saw Pia approaching the door.

"Hi, Pia," he said in the warmest tone.

"Hi, Mr. Raymond," Pia said, glistening with sweat as she began breathing slowly to catch her breath.

"You must be really working hard in there," he smiled.

"Yeah, with the internet down and school not fully functional, I have a lot of time to devote to dance," she explained.

"That's actually why I came over. I wanted to reach out with a proposition... an interview of sorts, if you're interested."

"What about?" she asked.

"The military, by way of the government, is doing some exploratory sessions to see how the internet is affecting society."

Pia paused, and Raymond held his breath, listening for any sign of suspicion in her voice. But when Pia replied, her tone was hesitant but curious.

"An interview?" she repeated. "I mean...sure. I think that could be interesting."

Raymond exhaled slowly, relief blending with a hint of regret. "Excellent," he said. "Let's set something up soon. I'm looking forward to it."

"Sure, just let me know when," Pia said.

"I'll be in touch," Raymond said and walked back toward the lodge, the reality of his decision settling over him. He'd taken the first step. There was no turning back now.

CHAPTER NINETEEN

"Pia, over here," Pierre waved Pia over to the table he and Rosa Jimenez were occupying.

Rosa was dressed in a pink floral sundress. The spring sun highlighting her skin. Her eyes smiled with glee that made Pia's heart sink. Pierre wore a light blue polo with linen pants and brown sandals. His smile made Pia feel even worse. She walked over to the table, smiling nervously.

"Hey, guys," Pia said.

"Come sit by me," Pierre said, patting the seat next to him. "I went ahead and ordered lemonade. Once Lilliana gets here, we'll order entrees."

"Great," Pia said dryly.

"It's so good seeing you, Pia. How have you been, you know, with the internet down and all?" Ms. Jimnez asked.

"It's been cool. I miss the convenience, of course, but I can't complain," Pia said.

"That's a positive outlook," Rosa said. "Most teenagers have been freaking out. Lil has definitely been acting crazy since it went down."

"How so?" Lilliana asked, visibly agitated.

The sudden interruption came from behind them. Lilliana had been standing there long enough to hear everything. Her mother's laughter felt like a slap, a mockery. *Crazy.* That word again. She was tired of it—tired of being misunderstood, dismissed, left out of decisions that shook her world.

Rosa's smile faltered, her entire face collapsing in slow motion. She turned and saw Lilliana standing stiffly, arms crossed, her eyes burning holes into the back of her head.[1]

"How so?" Lilliana repeated, louder this time, her voice sharp like broken glass. "Go ahead, finish what you were saying about your crazy daughter."

---

1. **Book Soundtrack Cue**: "Sandcastles" – Beyoncé.

"Lil…" Rosa's voice wavered. "Not today, please. Not right now—"

Lilliana stepped forward, her nostrils flaring. "You're unbelievable." Her gaze snapped to Pia. "And you—what are you even doing here?"

"Woah," Pia said, raising her hands. "I didn't mean anything—"

"Pierre…" Rosa started, taking a breath. "Let's just go ahead and tell her."

"No," Lilliana said. "No need. I'm sure I can guess," she said, keeping her eyes on Pia, who returned the favor.

Rosa stood up slowly, her eyes searching her daughter's face. "Lil, can you please just sit for a second—"

"Really, Mom?" Lilliana cut her off. "I'm going to be late for work."

"Lilliana," Pierre said carefully, "this is about your mom being happy—for once."

"Lilliana, wait—can we just talk for a minute?" Rosa's voice cracked, barely above a whisper. But her daughter was already turning away. She spun on her heel and stormed off, her heels clacking like gunshots against the pavement.

She used to run into my arms after school. Rosa thought. *Now she won't even meet my eyes.*

Pierre looked concerned as Rosa stared after her, visibly shaken.

"It's okay, baby," he said gently, stepping beside her. Rosa blinked rapidly, trying to dam the tears welling in her eyes. She pressed a trembling hand to her lips, as if trying to hold her heart in her chest.

"I thought she'd be happy for me..." she whispered, voice thick. "I just wanted to share this moment with her."

Pia placed a comforting hand on Rosa's. "She just needs time, Rosa. I can tell this means a lot to you."

Rosa nodded, but her eyes were glassy, distant. "She's all I have. I never thought... I never imagined she'd look at me like a stranger."

Pierre exhaled slowly, then opened the small box and turned it toward Pia and Rosa. Inside was a stunning pink diamond ring.

"We're engaged!!" Rosa said with a forced burst of excitement.

"Congratulations!!" Pia said, forcing enthusiasm. "I'm happy for you two."

"Thanks, Pia, that means a lot," Rosa said, teary-eyed.

Lilliana was furious by the time she made it to her car, rage swirling in her chest like a hurricane. She didn't want her mom to have anything to do with the Pierce's. She couldn't shake how Pia was looking at her all smug. She wanted nothing more than to get even.

She clenched her fists so tightly her nails dug crescents into her palms.

"Unbelievable," she muttered.

Lilliana climbed into her car and immediately began texting.

Lilliana: Hey, we need to talk…

Zaya: For what?

Lilliana: I haven't been myself lately and I owe you an apology. Just give me a chance to explain

Zaya: I'm listening

Lilliana: Meet me tonight at The Loft around 9

Zaya: I'll give you 5 mins

Lilliana: Thanks so much Za. That's all I need.

The dim lighting of The Loft cast shadows on the dark wood floors, creating an intimate atmosphere. Low hums of conversation and the occasional clink of glasses filled the air. Zaya slid into the booth across from Lilliana. Lilliana waved at the server and ordered drinks—a whiskey sour for herself and a mocktail for Zaya.

"Thanks for agreeing to meet me. There's so much I want to say, but I don't know where to start," Lilliana began.

Zaya frowned slightly, sensing a shift in the air. "Are you okay? Because that shit you pulled was not cool."

"I'm fine," Lilliana said through gritted teeth, her focus narrowing. She closed her eyes and muttered an incantation under her breath.

"What?" Zaya asked, looking confused.

The doll in Lilliana's hand grew warm, then hot, and she felt a surge of power ripple through her veins.

Across the table, Zaya gasped, clutching her chest. Her breath hitched, and her eyes widened in panic. "Lilliana... what's happening?"

Lilliana's eyes snapped open, blazing with triumph. "It's finally working," she whispered.

Zaya doubled over, her hand trembling as she gripped the edge of the table. Sweat beaded on her forehead, and her lips moved, forming words Lilliana couldn't hear.

But just as quickly as it began, the energy fizzled. The doll in Lilliana's hand grew cold, lifeless once more. However, the damage was done. Zaya was lying unconscious. Lilliana quickly threw the doll in her purse.

"Help! Somebody help me!" Lilliana screamed as she began shaking Zaya to wake her up. Lilliana managed to drop a few tears. "Please, somebody call 911!!" Lilliana held her head down in what seemed to be in prayer, her lips curving into a small, calculated smile.

Several patrons ran over, one attempting CPR.

"She has a pulse," one guy said. "We need an ambulance."

After Zaya was loaded into the back of the ambulance, Lilliana disappeared from the scene. She didn't want to answer any questions, fearing what Zaya might remember if she lived.

I have to get this under control! Lilliana thought. She drove off to meet Blaze, irritated that Zaya was still breathing.

The sky was an eerie gray, and street lights flickered sporadically, the power grid struggling to keep up with the unusual demands caused by the city-wide internet outage.

He stood at the corner of Lindbergh Street. His crew was scattered around him, a dozen figures moving like predators in the night, their laughter low and sinister as they scoped out the neighborhood.

"This place is ripe for the taking," Blaze said, his voice smooth but laced with malice. He gestured to the rows of dimly lit homes, their residents oblivious to the lurking danger.

"Yeah, no alarms, no calls for help," sneered Foogi, Blaze's right-hand man. He spun a crowbar in his hand like a toy. "They're sitting ducks."

Blaze smirked, his golden eyes glinting in the faint light. "Keep it clean and quick. No witnesses. And if they try to get smart..." He let the sentence trail off, but the wicked grin that followed said enough.

The crew moved into action, spreading out in pairs. Windows were pried open, and doors were forced without the telltale hum of security systems. In one house, a young couple cowered as two masked crew members rummaged through their belongings, pocketing jewelry and cash.

"Please, just take what you want and go," the man begged, shielding his wife.

"Shut up," one of the intruders barked, slamming the man against the wall. "You're lucky we're feeling generous tonight."

Outside, Blaze walked the streets like a king surveying his domain. He stopped in front of a modest corner house where the lights were still on. A teenage boy peeked out from behind the curtains, his face pale and frightened.

Blaze tilted his head, amused. "Foogi, we've got a curious one."

Foogi looked up from smashing the headlights of a parked car. "Want me to handle it?"

Blaze held up a hand. "Nah. Let's give him a show." He turned to the boy, his voice loud enough to carry. "You think staying inside makes you safe, bitch ass nigga? You think your little hiding spot means we can't get to you?"

The boy's eyes widened, and the curtain fell back into place.

Blaze laughed, a sound devoid of humor. "Exactly what I thought."

A commotion down the street drew his attention., Axel, one of the newer recruits, was dragging a man out of his car, her blade glinting in the faint light. The man pleaded, his hands raised in surrender.

"Good work," Blaze said as he approached. "Take the car."

The man whimpered, but Blaze didn't spare him another glance.

Within the hour, the neighborhood was a patchwork of shattered windows, overturned trash cans, and empty driveways. Blaze and his crew regrouped at the edge of the block, their bags heavy with stolen goods and their laughter echoing through the hollow silence.

Blaze looked back at the darkened neighborhood, his expression one of smug satisfaction. "Let's move. We've got more ground to cover."

As they disappeared into the night, the sound of distant sirens finally pierced the still air—but by then, Blaze and his crew were long gone.

Pia woke up the next morning to her dad knocking aggressively on her door.

"Yeah, dad, what's wrong?" Pia said as her heart was racing from being abruptly awakened.

Pierre swung the door open. "Sweet pea, I'm afraid I have some bad news."

"What is it?" Pia asked. She sat up in her bed, anxiously awaiting his response.

"Well, first, I want you to know that things are getting bad. I don't want you out late at all. A gang devastated Shadow Ridge last night. They broke into houses, stole all kinds of things, and even assaulted a few people."

Pia's eyes widened as she listened.

"Are you serious, dad? What are the police saying?"

"They didn't get there in time and no one is talking. People are scared and they have every right to be. So, I want you home by 8 pm. No excuses, Pia."

"Okay, dad, I get it. I'll make sure I'm home," Pia said solemnly.

"Good...and there's something else."

"What is it?" Pia asked hesitantly.

"Zaya's mom dropped by this morning. Zaya is in the hospital. The doctors aren't sure what happened, but she was unconscious last night."

Pia jumped out of bed, throwing on a pair of jeans that lay on the floor. She slid on Nike's with no socks.

"No one knows what happened. She was hanging out with Lilliana and no one has seen her either," Pierre said helplessly as he watched his daughter move frantically around the room.

"I have to go see her dad. I have to go," Pia said, walking into the living room.

"I understand," Pierre followed. "There's a town hall meeting today at 2 pm. I was hoping you would go back with me."

"Of course. I'm canceling classes today. Zaya needs me." *And this town does too, Pia thought.*

CHAPTER TWENTY

T he crowd in the town hall was restless, their voices a chaotic
mix of anger and fear. The mayor, with tired eyes, stood at
the podium, her attempts to maintain order drowned out by the
uproar.

"Order! Order, please!" she shouted, banging the gavel on the
wooden stand.

"Order?" someone yelled from the back. "You mean like the order
we *don't* have in Windsorville?"

The crowd erupted in agreement. Pierre stood against the wall, his
arms crossed over his chest. Although he and Pia arrived at 1:45,
the room was packed.

"Mayor Jenkins," a woman in a business suit said, stepping forward. She adjusted her glasses and spoke with a shaky voice. "I

own the diner on Fourth Street. It's my livelihood, and now it's in shambles because the gangs trashed it two nights ago. Where were the police when this happened? Where *are* they now?"

"We're trying," the mayor said weakly.

"Your best isn't enough!" Pierre's voice cut through the room, deep and firm. The room turned to him as he stepped forward, his presence commanding attention.

"The gangs aren't just vandalizing. They're hurt people, and I have a daughter I have to protect. Where are the soldiers? If they're not going to help, what are they here for?" Pierre

Murmurs of discontent rippled through the crowd. Pia gulped. She'd never seen her dad or her community like this—fractured, furious, and desperate. Not only did she have to worry about Lilliana, but Blaze and his crew had taken everything people thought was safe and turned it to ash, and now the internet outage had left the town isolated and vulnerable.

"And it's not just me," Pierre continued, his tone growing angrier. "It's all of us. Businesses, homes, families—no one's safe. We can't sit here and wait for help that's never coming."

A man in a plaid shirt stood up. "Pierre's right! We're the ones who have to live here, not them. We can't rely on the police anymore."

"What do you suggest we do?" someone else called out.

A man from the back, wearing a leather jacket, spoke up. "We protect our own. We band together—neighbors watching out for neighbors. Patrols, check-ins, whatever it takes to keep the gangs out of our neighborhoods. They want to scare us into hiding, but we're stronger together."

The room was silent for a moment, then the woman from the diner nodded. "He's right. They can't take us all on if we stand together."

The mayor looked pale, her gavel forgotten in her hand. "Now, wait a minute," she stammered. "Vigilantism isn't the answer. The police—"

"The police aren't here!" someone shouted, cutting her off.

The man in a leather jacket spoke again. "I say we organize. Set up shifts for patrols. Start a network to keep each other informed. If something goes down, we're there to stop it before it gets out of hand."

Pierre nodded. "And we make it clear—this is *our* home. We don't bow to any gang or anyone else. We fight back."

The crowd erupted in applause and cheers, a spark of hope igniting in the air. People began shouting suggestions, volunteering for patrols, and exchanging phone numbers.

"Hey, Pia," Abel yelled across the parking lot as she and Pierre climbed into his truck.

"Hey, Abel," Pia waved.

Abel trotted over, out of breath. "Hi, Mr. Pierce," Abel said.

Pierre gave him a nod.

"Pia, I've been looking for you everywhere. I heard about Zaya, and I was about to head to the hospital."

"I visited her earlier today. She's actually fine, thank God! When I went to see her, she was awake and talking up a storm."

"Did she say what happened?"

"She couldn't remember. The doctors think she may have blacked out because of stress or something. They're keeping her for observation, but if there aren't any more problems, she could get discharged tomorrow."

"We could go back later tonight," Abel offered.

"I'm kind of on a curfew until the craziness calms down," Pia said.

"You should stay inside too," Pierre told Abel. "These gangs are out of control."

"Well, there's a candlelight vigil in the park tonight for the guy that was killed a few nights ago. I had planned on going, but I won't stay long."

"Dad, can we go?" Pia asked. "United front, you know?"

"Only for a few minutes," Pierre sighed.

"Cool! I'll meet y'all there," Abel said, slapping the roof off Pierre's truck.

Pia and Pierre drove off in silence, Pierre deep in thought while Pia looked out the window.

"Dad," Pia began, "I had no idea how upset you were about everything."

"I already lost your mom. I can't lose you, too," Pierre said quietly.

Pia leaned over and lay her head against his shoulder while he drove. She understood.

The sun began to set as a crowd filled Windsorville Park. It seemed to be a big turnout. The soft glow of hundreds of candles illuminated the park. Pia, Pierre, and Abel stood close together near the front, their hands cupping the candles as they protected them from the gentle evening breeze. The once-vibrant park seemed somber, cloaked in the heavy grief of the townspeople.

Balloons and a portrait of Kendrix Mason were centered in the gazebo in the middle of the park. Kendrix Mason was a well-known businessman who owned an accounting firm downtown. He was murdered while being robbed at his office. People would step forward and say a few kind words, and then step back so the next person could speak. Finally, Jackson Marks, owner of the town's hardware store, cleared his throat.

"We need to be each other's eyes and ears," he said. "Kendrix used to say that a strong community is like a sturdy fence—you patch up the weak spots before they turn into holes. Let's set up groups to check on each other, especially at night."

Nods of agreement rippled through the crowd.

Nadia Rivera, who ran the community center, raised her voice. "Jackson's right, but we also need to figure out how to communicate without the internet. What if we set up a message board in town? A physical one—where people can leave updates, share information, or just check in."

An older man called out, "And what about radios? We still have a CB setup at the fire station. We could train people to use it, keep lines open for emergencies."

Pastor Green stepped forward, his hands clasped in front of him. "We also need to keep our spirits strong. My church hall is open for gatherings—whether for planning or just to talk and support each other. Kendrix believed in this community, and we have to hold on to that belief."

A ripple of hope began to replace the tension in the air as hands went up, offering help. The townsfolk began organizing into smaller groups. Pia looked up at her dad smiling, but then she saw terror on his face.

Bang! Bang! Bang! Bang! Bang! Bang!

A deafening crack split the air, and panic erupted in an instant. People screamed and dove for cover as more shots followed, rapid and relentless. The once-peaceful park was now a battleground.

From the edge of the park, a group of men emerged, their figures silhouetted against the glow of the streetlights. At the front was Blaze, a twisted grin on his face. Behind him, his crew carried assault rifles with extended clips.

Blaze fired a shot into the air, his voice booming over the chaos. "You think candles and prayers will stop us? We are the new order!"

Pia and Pierre fled to the other side of the gazebo, ducking and peering out.

A woman screamed as one of the crew kicked over a table, scattering candles and flowers. Another man grabbed a teen by the collar, slamming him into the ground. Fights broke out as some of the braver residents tried to defend themselves, but Blaze's crew was heavily armed and merciless.

Abel, who had been standing near the memorial, clenched his fists. "We can't let them destroy this!" he shouted, rushing forward to protect a woman who had fallen. Pia looked through the gazebo just in time to see a gun being drawn from Abel's waist. As she screamed, *no*, he fired a shot at one of the crew members, striking Mr. Marks.

Abel's hands trembled as he stared at the weapon. He hadn't meant to hurt anyone. "Mr. Marks... I didn't—"

Pia rushed over to Mr. Marks with Pierre on her heel, only to see that it was a flesh wound. Abel stood there, frozen in fear of actually hurting someone innocent. Pia saw the crew member who Abel tried to shoot aim his gun in Abel's direction, bearing a skull in fire tattoo just like Blaze's.

"Abel, get down!" Pia screamed.

The bullet whizzed past Abel, striking the Gazebo where Pia and Pierre once hid. *This is getting out of hand*, Pia thought. *I have to do something.*

Nadia Rivera pulled a small group of teenagers behind a bench, shielding them as bullets zipped past. "Stay low!" she hissed, her heart pounding.

Blaze's crew continued their rampage, firing shots into the air and at the ground to keep people disoriented. One of the gang members spotted Pastor Green trying to lead a group of elderly residents to safety and aimed his weapon.

"No!" someone screamed.

Before the gang member could fire, a young man from the crowd tackled him, knocking the weapon loose. The two scuffled, rolling in the dirt as the townspeople watched in horror.

Blaze noticed the resistance and snarled. "You think you're heroes? You're all just fools waiting to get crushed!" He raised his rifle, aiming it toward Jackson, who was still helping the fallen woman.

Pia stood still, her dark eyes narrowing. Her hands clenched into fists, a soft glow beginning to emanate from her body. The light pulsed in her chest, hot and electric. Pia's hands shook as the glow spread to her fingertips. Her heart thudded—not from fear, but recognition. Something deep within her had awakened. She spotted Blaze, and without thinking, Pia launched forward with a blinding punch, sending him flying across the park. [1]

"Everyone get down," Pia screamed. The glow around her grew brighter, illuminating the darkness.

---

1. **Book Soundtrack Cue**: "We Gon' Be Alright" – Tye Tribbett.

She hurled one of the energy blasts toward a gang member trying to reload his weapon. It exploded on impact, sending him sprawling and disarming him instantly. Another orb followed, creating a barrier of light between Blaze's crew and the townspeople still trying to escape.

Blaze growled, raising his rifle. He fired, but the bullets couldn't penetrate the orb.

"Pia, where are you?" Pierre called out in a panic. Pierre tried to look Pia's way, but he was blinded by the light.

Pia raised her hands again, summoning a massive blast that floated above her head, pulsating with energy. With a sweeping motion, she sent it rolling toward the gang like a tidal wave. The blast engulfed them, its energy knocking their weapons from their hands and pinning them to the ground. The men were hurt, groaning in pain on the ground.

The townspeople began to emerge from their hiding spots.

"Pia, where did you go? I couldn't find you," Pierre said as he found Pia kneeling to the ground.

"I don't know what happened. I saw a light, and I got down," Pia explained, drained and short of breath.

Abel walked up, looking at Pia peculiarly.

"Abel, what were you doing with a gun?" Pierre asked, pulling Pia up on her feet.

"I didn't want to be left defenseless. I promised myself I wouldn't get hurt again," Abel said. "But clearly, I didn't need it."

"What happened here tonight was strange," Pierre admitted.

"Thankfully, Mr. Marks will be okay," Pia said.

There was an awkward silence that lingered for a minute.

"Abel, can you help Pia to the truck? I'm going to check around to see if anyone needs help."

"Sure, Mr. Pierce."

Pia and Abel made their way to the truck, walking in silence. Pia, feeling exhausted, climbed into the passenger side and immediately let the seat back.

"Long night, huh?" Abel said, eyes lingering on Pia.

"Why are you looking at me like that?" Pia asked.

"Just trying to make sure you're okay. That's all."

"I'm fine. You can go back and help my dad. I'll be okay," Pia sighed.

"Sure. Just one more thing."

"What?" Pia said, impatiently.

"You could've trusted me with your secret."

Pia's eyes widened as Abel slammed the door and headed back towards the park. She stared at the back of his silhouette, speechless and terrified.

CHAPTER TWENTY-ONE

The Masonic Lodge loomed ahead, its darkened windows staring like hollow eyes. Pia tightened her grip on the wheel, her pulse ticking louder than the car's engine. She hadn't slept in days. Her dad kept hovering, Abel had ghosted her, and Nolan's messages came in like ghosts through a flickering signal. Still, she promised Raymond.

Pia parked her car and stepped out. Something about the place felt...off.

She stood at the large wooden door and knocked. Moments later, the door creaked open, and Raymond appeared.

"Pia! Glad you could make it," he said, motioning her inside.

As Pia crossed the threshold, something inside her shuddered. The air was wrong—too still, too heavy. Her fingertips tingle like static crawling under her skin. Pia stepped in cautiously, her eyes scanning the grand but eerily silent hall. The walls were adorned with faded tapestries, and the air smelled faintly of aged wood and incense.

He gestured toward a room off the main hall with a table and chairs set up in the center of the room. A tape recorder and notepad sat on the table, along with a pitcher of water and two glasses.

"Shall we?" he said, pulling out a chair for her.

Pia sat, setting her belongings on the table. As Raymond took his seat across from her, she studied his face. Something in his demeanor was... different. The easy confidence was still there, but there was an edge to it, a sharpness in his eyes that put her on edge.

He pressed record on the tape recorder. "Let's get started. Can you share your perspective on how it's impacting Windsorville specifically?"

Pia nodded and began speaking, her words measured and thoughtful. But as she talked, she noticed subtle shifts in Raymond's posture. He wasn't just listening—he was studying her. His eyes darted to her hands, her face, her body language, as if searching for something.

When she paused, he leaned forward, his tone probing. "And what about you, Pia? You've changed since the blackout."

"Changed how?"

"Some people glow when the lights go out."

Pia's instincts flared. She felt a faint hum in the air—a subtle vibration she recognized all too well. Her powers responded to it, flickering to life beneath her skin.

"What's really going on, Raymond?" Pia said, her voice cold.

"You're smarter than I gave you credit for," he said, standing up.

A low hum filled the air, and she saw the faint glow of devices embedded in the walls—energy sensors calibrated to her.

"You've been hiding something, Pia," Raymond said, his voice calm but menacing. "I've been tracking energy spikes since the blackout started, and they all lead to you. After what happened in your studio, I just needed you in the right place to test my theory."

Pia stood, her hands glowing faintly as her power surged. "You set me up."

Raymond stepped back, raising his hands as if to placate her. "It's not personal. But someone with abilities like yours? You're wasting it hiding in this town. I have people—powerful people—who'd be very interested in what you can do. I just need you to come with me."

"You're not taking me anywhere."

Raymond smirked and pressed a button on a remote. From the shadows, two large figures stepped forward, their faces obscured by masks.

The first figure raised a strange-looking weapon, firing at Pia.

The blast missed her by inches. Heat scorched her cheek as the chair vaporized. She dove behind the table, rolled, and struck—her fist like a meteor, her power rippling the floor like a quake.

The second figure charged her, but she met him with a punch that sent him sprawling. Her strength rippled through the room, shaking the ground.

Raymond moved toward the exit, but Pia turned, her voice ringing out. "You're not going anywhere, Raymond." She raised her hands, creating a glowing barrier that blocked the door.

He froze, panic flickering across his face. "You don't understand, Pia. If you don't come willingly, they'll send others. You can't run from this."

Raymond stood near the wall, his hand trembling slightly as he gripped the strange device he'd been using to disable Pia's powers. The masked men lay unconscious around the room, but Pia's glowing hands told him she wasn't finished yet.

"You should've thought twice before trying to set me up," Pia said, her voice sharp and steady.

Before Raymond could respond, the sound of heavy footsteps echoed from the hall, followed by a familiar voice.

There was a crash outside the room, and Pia looked towards the door, fearing more people were coming to take her.

"Pia!" Nolan's voice cut through the chaos.

She turned to see Nolan, his broad frame silhouetted in the doorway. His expression shifted from confusion to fury as he took in the scene—Raymond cowering, the unconscious enforcers, and Pia glowing with barely restrained energy.

"Nolan?" Pia said, her voice softening for a moment.

"What the hell is going on here?" Nolan demanded, striding into the room.

Raymond straightened, trying to regain his composure. "Nolan, you don't understand—this isn't what it looks like."

Nolan's jaw tightened. "It looks like you're trying to hurt my girlfriend."

Pia stepped back slightly, her glowing hands dimming as she looked between the two men. She had never seen Nolan like this—his usual calm demeanor replaced by raw anger.

Raymond hesitated, then pointed at Pia. "She's a Nuru, Nolan."

"A what?" Nolan said, confused.

"I know you don't know what that means, but she's dangerous. If we don't act now, others will come for her. I was trying to protect all of us."

Nolan's eyes narrowed. "Protect us? From what? I know Pia!"

Raymond's defiance faltered, but he tried again. "You don't get it. She's powerful. If we don't—"

"Enough!" Nolan roared, cutting him off. He turned to Pia, his expression softening. "Are you okay? I saw your car parked over here, then I heard the sounds. I didn't know what was going on."

"I'm okay, Nolan. I'm soooo happy to see you. I don't know where he was trying to take me."

Raymond tried to edge toward the door, but Nolan moved quickly, grabbing him by the arm and slamming him against the wall. Nolan pulled out his phone to call 911, but the call didn't seem to go through.

Nolan glanced at her, his expression softening despite the anger that had clouded his features moments ago. "We'll figure this out, Pia. I promise."

She nodded, her voice caught in her throat. She wanted to believe him—to hold on to the calm strength he always radiated—but the unease in her heart wouldn't settle.

A sudden noise behind them—a scuffle, a clatter—snapped them both to attention. Pia spun around, her powers sparking instinctively in her hands.

Raymond stood in the doorway of the lodge, his face twisted with desperation and rage. In his hands, he clutched one of the strange energy weapons his enforcers had used earlier, its barrel glowing faintly.

"You think you can just walk away from this?" he snarled. His voice was unhinged, the calm mask he usually wore completely shattered.

"Raymond, don't do this," Nolan said, stepping in front of Pia protectively.

"Stay out of this, Nolan! Her kind killed my father!" Raymond shouted, raising the weapon. His hands trembled, but his aim was steady.

Before Pia could react, the world erupted in light and sound. A sharp, deafening crack split the air as Raymond pulled the trigger.

The energy blast hit Nolan square in the chest, and he staggered, his eyes wide with shock. He turned toward Pia, his hand reaching out as he collapsed to the ground.[1]

---

1. **Book Soundtrack Cue**: "Rescue" – Lauren Daigle.

"Nolan!" Pia screamed, dropping to her knees beside him.

His breathing was shallow, his eyes struggling to focus on her. "Pia..." he whispered, his voice barely audible. Then his body went still, the light fading from his eyes.

For a moment, the world seemed to stop. Pia's breath came in ragged gasps as the reality of what had just happened crashed down on her. Tears blurred her vision, and a raw, guttural cry tore from her throat. She screamed so loud all the glass in the lodge shattered. The lodge shook as cracks ran through the walls. The glow in her hands flared, brighter and more volatile than ever before.

"You killed him!" she roared, standing and turning toward Raymond.

The surrounding air shimmered with energy as orbs of light formed in her hands, crackling with power. She hurled the first one at him; the explosion sent shards of wood and stone flying as it hit the doorway where he'd been standing.

Raymond stumbled back, panic in his eyes. "You don't understand, Pia! This isn't over!"

She hurled another blast, narrowly missing him as he darted behind a corner. The ground shook as her power surged uncontrollably, her vision blurring with rage.

"Come back here!" she screamed, her voice echoing through the lodge.

But Raymond was gone, disappearing into the shadows.

Pia stood there, her chest heaving, the energy around her flickering and fading as her anger gave way to overwhelming grief. She sank to her knees beside Nolan's lifeless body, her hands trembling as she touched his face.

"I'm so sorry," she whispered, her tears falling freely now. "I'm so sorry, Nolan."

The night was silent again; the stillness was only broken by Pia's quiet sobs as she cradled him, the weight of her loss crashing down on her.

CHAPTER TWENTY-TWO

P ia sat on the couch in the living room, her knees drawn to her chest. As her thoughts flashed over the last 12 hours, the faint scent of his cologne brought fresh waves of pain with every breath.[1]

Pierre sat in the recliner across from her. He didn't speak much. Instead, he was there, his presence a quiet anchor in the storm of her grief. He sipped his coffee slowly, his eyes fixed on the floor, giving Pia space but ready to step in if she needed him. The faint knock at the door broke the silence. Pierre glanced at Pia, but she didn't move.

"I'll get it," he said, setting his mug on the side table and shuffling to the door.

---

1. **Book Soundtrack Cue**: "Free Mind" – Tems.

When he opened it, Zaya stood on the porch, holding a small bouquet of wildflowers. Her face etched with concern.

"Hi, Mr. Pierce," she whispered. "I came to see Pia."

He nodded and stepped aside. "She's in the living room."

Zaya entered, her gaze immediately landing on her friend.

"P," she said gently, kneeling beside the couch.

Pia didn't look up, her tear-streaked face partially hidden behind her arms. Zaya placed a hand on her shoulder, squeezing lightly. "I'm so sorry, Pia. I don't even know what to say."

At the sound of Zaya's voice, Pia's composure crumbled. A sob escaped her lips, and she buried her face in her hands. "He's gone, Zaya," she choked out. "Nolan's...gone. And it's my fault."

Zaya's eyes welled with tears as she wrapped her arms around Pia, gripping her. "No, P. Don't do that to yourself. This isn't on you."

Pia shook her head, her voice breaking. "If I hadn't gone to the lodge... If I'd just been smarter... maybe he'd still be here."

Zaya pulled back slightly, her hands resting on Pia's shoulders. "You can't do this, Pia. No one knew the Raymond guy was a lunatic."

Pierre cleared his throat, his voice steady. "Zaya's right. Nolan made his choices because he cared about you. Sometimes life's unfair like that, but you can't let it break you."

Pia wiped her eyes, looking between them. "I don't know how to move past this."

"Give it time, Pia. Me, Abel, your dad...we've got you."

Pierre nodded, his steady gaze meeting Pia's. "We'll get through this together. You're not alone."

"Right, you couldn't get rid of us if you tried," Zaya added, grabbing a kleenex off of the table and blotting Pia's tears.

Zaya slid onto the couch next to Pia, holding her hand. The pair sat there in silence. Understanding what didn't need to be said.

The sun had gone down. Zaya stood at the door, her hand resting on the frame as she turned back to look at Pia.

"I'll be back to check on you tomorrow," Zaya said gently.

Pia nodded, managing a faint smile. "Thanks, Zaya. For everything."

"You just rest, P. I've got a few things I want to look into anyway."

Zaya gave her a quick hug before stepping outside. As she walked down the steps, a car pulled into the driveway. Zaya squinted at the headlights until the engine shut off and Abel stepped out.

Abel waited until she drove off before making his way to the door, his hands stuffed in his jacket pockets. Pia stood in the doorway, peering at him through tight, puffy eyes.

"Hey," he mumbled.

"Hey," Pia replied, her voice barely above a whisper. She stepped aside to let him in.

The silence between them was heavy as Abel entered the living room. Pierre had gone to bed, leaving the house quiet save for the faint hum of the refrigerator in the kitchen.

"I heard about Nolan," Abel said, his voice low and measured. He hesitated, then reached out to touch her arm. "I'm so sorry, Pia."

Her eyes filled with tears, and she nodded, unable to speak. Abel pulled her into a hug, holding her as she cried against his chest. His arms were strong and steady, grounding her as waves of grief washed over her again.

When she finally pulled back, she wiped her face, giving him a watery smile. "Thanks for coming."

"Of course," he said, his tone gentle. But as he looked at her, his expression shifted, a flicker of something unresolved crossing his face.

"Pia," he began, his voice tightening. "We need to talk."

She stiffened, her gaze dropping to the floor. "About the park?"

"Yeah." He stepped back, adjusting the brim of his fitted cap. "I saw what you did, the way your hands—" He paused, shaking his head. "I don't even know how to explain it."

Pia crossed her arms, her shoulders tense. "Abel, I wanted to tell you, but I didn't know how. I didn't want to put you in danger."

"Danger?" he repeated, frustration edging his voice. "Pia, I'm your best friend. We're supposed to have each other's backs, no matter what. Don't you think I deserved to know something this big about you? You let me talk about Nurus like I was a fool. You could have told me then."

"I know," she blurted, her voice breaking. "I know, and I'm sorry. But you saw what happened to Nolan. This is exactly why I didn't want to tell anyone. The more people know, the more they're at risk."

Abel's frustration softened as he saw the anguish in her eyes. He exhaled deeply, his tone gentler. "I get it, Pia. I do. I've been your friend since we were kids, and I'm not going anywhere. Powers or not, danger or not—I'm here."

Her lip quivered as she looked up at him. "You're not mad?"

He chuckled dryly. "Oh, I'm mad. But not because of your powers. I'm mad because you didn't trust me enough to let me help you. But I'll get over it."

Pia managed a small smile. "You're a good friend."

"So are you... a strong friend," Abel said firmly. "You're going through hell, and you're still standing. That takes strength, Pia. Even without the whole superhero thing."

She laughed softly; the sound was tinged with sadness. "Superhero, huh? I don't feel like one."

"Maybe not," he said, his tone thoughtful. "But you're the closest thing this town's got. And for what it's worth, I've got your back. Whatever you need."

Pia felt the weight on her chest ease, just a little. She reached out, squeezing his hand. "Thank you, Abel. That means everything to me."

He nodded, his grip firm and reassuring. "We'll figure this out. Together."

As they sat down on the couch, the room felt a little less empty, and for the first time in what felt like forever, Pia didn't feel completely alone.

The next morning came with Pia and Abel sprawled across the couch. They had ended the night watching old DVD movies. The scent of freshly brewed coffee drifted through the house, gently pulling Pia from the depths of her restless sleep. She blinked against the soft morning light filtering through her curtains, the faint sound of a spoon clinking against a mug echoing from the kitchen.

In the kitchen, Pierre stood at the counter pouring coffee into two mismatched mugs. He glanced over his shoulder when he heard her enter, his face lighting up with a small smile.

"Morning, sleepyhead," he said, sliding a mug toward her.

"Morning," she mumbled, taking the mug and wrapping her hands around it. The warmth seeped into her palms, grounding her.

"I figured I would fix some coffee, seeing how tired you and Abel were. I don't know which of you snored the loudest."

Pia chuckled, taking a seat at the breakfast table.

"I know yesterday was heavy on you, but I have some other news I want to share," Pierre said.

"What's going on, dad?" Pia asked.

"Rosa. She's pretty upset. Lilliana left late last night—moved back to New Orleans."

Pia froze mid-sip, carefully lowering the mug to keep her reaction in check. "Oh," she said, her voice as neutral as she could make it. "That's... sudden."

"Yeah," Pierre agreed, rubbing the back of his neck. "Rosa's been taking it hard. She kept saying she didn't see it coming."

Pia nodded, biting the inside of her cheek to keep the wave of relief from showing on her face.

"I'm sorry Rosa's upset," Pia said carefully, taking another sip of coffee. "I mean, Lilliana's always been kind of unpredictable, right? Maybe she just needed a change."

Marcus nodded slowly, his expression thoughtful. "Maybe. But she could've at least talked to Rosa about it first. Just up and leaving like that? Feels off."

"I hope there's enough for me," Abel said from the living room. He sat on the couch, stretching his legs.

"This is some good coffee, Dad," Pia said, cradling her mug with both hands.

"You're welcome," Pierre replied with a satisfied grin. "I may not be a barista, but I know my way around a coffee pot."

Abel chuckled, stretching still. "You've got my vote for best coffee in town."

The faint chime of Pia's phone from the counter interrupted the peaceful atmosphere. She frowned, exchanging a curious glance with Abel.

"Did your phone just go off?" Abel asked, raising an eyebrow.

"Yeah," she said, standing to grab it.

As she unlocked the screen, her phone vibrated again. And again. Notifications flooded her device. At the same time, Abel's phone buzzed in his pocket, and Pierre's sat blinking on the table.

"What the—" Pierre said, reaching for his phone.

Before any of them could react, their screens dimmed, and a message appeared, stark white text on a black background:

"THE INTERNET HAS BEEN RESTORED UNDER STRICT REGULATIONS FOR THE SAFETY OF THE AMERICAN PEOPLE. ACCESS TO CERTAIN FEATURES HAS BEEN LIMITED TO ENSURE STABILITY AND SECURITY. ANY ATTEMPT TO CIRCUMVENT THESE MEASURES WILL BE MET WITH IMMEDIATE ACTION."

Pia's stomach tightened as she scrolled down. Below the message was a smaller line of text:

"FOR PUBLIC SAFETY, ALL USERS WILL BE MONITORED. NON-COMPLIANCE IS PROHIBITED."

"What the hell is this?" Abel said, his voice sharp.

Pierre frowned, setting his phone down. "Restrictions? What are they talking about? They're treating the internet like it's a privilege instead of a service."

Pia glanced at Abel, whose face was tight with concern. Her mind raced, piecing together the unsettling puzzle.

The phones buzzed again. This time, a series of app icons grayed out, replaced by a lock symbol.

Abel leaned closer, his voice hushed. "You think this is about...*that.*"

"Maybe," Pia said, swallowing hard.

Abel touched her arm, grounding her. "We'll figure this out," he whispered, though his eyes betrayed his worry.

Pia's mind raced with questions. The internet was back, but it felt like freedom had disappeared altogether. As she stared at her phone, something caught her eye.

A new app.

Its icon was simple—a gray T icon on an orange background with no text or label. She frowned, tilting her phone to inspect it as if the angle might reveal more.

"Where the hell did you come from?" she muttered.

She tapped the icon, but nothing happened. The screen didn't load, nor did the app open. Instead, it seemed to pulse faintly, a slow flicker of light that made her phone feel heavier in her hand.

Pia shuddered and held down the icon to delete it. When the "Remove App" option appeared, she pressed it quickly.

But nothing happened. The app remained motionless yet eerily present.

"What is this?" she whispered.

"Dad, Abel," she called, holding up her phone. "Do you see this app on your phone?"

They both looked up, their faces puzzled.

"App?" Pierre asked.

Pia handed him her phone. "This one. It just appeared. A gray T icon on an orange background."

Pierre squinted, scrolling through her screen. Then he looked at his. "Yeah, I do actually. Haven't seen anything like this on mine."

Abel reached for his own phone, unlocking it and quickly swiping through his home screen. "Same here," he said, glancing up at her. "What is this?"

Pia felt a chill crawl up her spine. "I don't know," she said, sitting down beside them.

"Maybe it's some weird glitch," Pierre offered, though his tone wasn't confident.

Abel frowned, leaning closer to her. "A glitch doesn't stop you from deleting it. And why is it showing up now?"

Her heart pounded as she exchanged a glance with Abel.

"Maybe we should go to the store tomorrow and have someone look at our phones," Pierre said.

"No," Pia said quickly, gripping her phone. "I mean... let me figure it out first. It might be nothing."

Her dad eyed her suspiciously, but nodded. "Alright. Just let me know if anything else happens, okay?"

"I will," she promised.

Pia stared at the faintly pulsing app, dread pooling in her stomach. She needed some air.

CHAPTER TWENTY-THREE

Pia stepped onto Marie's porch, her knock barely louder than the crickets' song. The sun had long since set, leaving the world painted in deep blues and grays. In her chest, the weight of grief pressed heavily, an unyielding reminder of Nolan's absence.

The door was ajar, candlelight spilling onto the front steps.

"Come in, child," Ms. Marie beckoned.

Pia hesitated for a moment, gathering herself, before stepping inside. Marie stood by the fireplace, her silver-streaked hair pulled into a loose braid. Her eyes, piercing yet kind, met Pia's. Tay lay in a recliner near the fire, snug under a blanket with his eyes closed, yet a smile spread across his face.

"I knew you would come when you were ready. I'm sorry for what you've had to endure," Marie spoke gently.

"I don't want to be afraid or unprepared for anyone or anything that comes my way. I *definitely* won't lose anyone else that I care about," she said.

Pia sank into the armchair across from Marie, her hands resting limply in her lap. Her voice cracked under the weight of her emotions. "I need to know... what it means to be Nuru. To fully embrace it."

Marie studied her for a moment, then leaned forward. "Do you understand what you're asking, child? Stepping into your Nuru self is not just about power. It's about transformation. About pain. And about choosing who you will become."

"I've lost Nolan," Pia said, her voice trembling. "I've lost so much," she thought of her mother—the loss still raw, another wound she carried. "But I'm still here. If this pain means I can become stronger—so I can protect others—then I'm ready."

Marie's gaze softened. "Your transformation is already happening so quickly."

Pia frowned. "Transformation?"

Marie nodded, rising to retrieve an old, leather-bound book from the shelf. She opened it, revealing intricate sketches of winged beings and shimmering creatures. "There are stages to becoming a Nuru," she explained. "We are not born into our full strength. Each stage reflects not just power, but the depth of our souls. Pain speeds up the process, but only if you keep your heart untainted by hatred or vengeance."

"I want understanding... and my friends and family to be safe."

"Then listen closely," Marie said, her voice dropping into a reverent whisper. "You are moving beyond the first stage, where your abilities awaken. The second stage—where you are now—heightens your connection to the Essence. Your senses will sharpen, your powers will grow, and you'll begin to see the threads that bind this world together."

"And beyond that?" Pia asked.

Marie hesitated, her fingers trailing over the book's pages. "Few reach the final stage. It is the stage—" Marie hesitated, "A state of unparalleled wisdom and power. But it comes at great cost."

"What's the cost?" Pia asked, intrigued.

Marie smiled faintly. "Not all ascend that far. For now, focus on the path before you. Let your pain guide you, but not define you."

"What are you not telling me, Marie?"

"Marie, huh? Okay. Well, how about I show you?" Marie spoke earnestly.

"I'm sorry, Ms. Marie. I haven't been myself. But yes, I *do* want to know. Show me. I'm ready."[1]

"Come, follow me," Marie instructed.

Pia followed closely behind Marie, the click of their footsteps echoing down the damp stone staircase. The air grew cooler with each step, and the faint scent of earth and mildew tickled Pia's nose. She shivered as a drop of moisture splashed onto her cheek, running down her jawline like a cold tear.

They reached the bottom of the stairs, and Pia hesitated. The hallway stretched endlessly before her, the only light coming from flickering torches mounted on the damp stone walls. Enormous, iron-bound doors lined the corridor, each adorned with intricate carvings that seemed to shift and writhe when she looked at them for too long.

"Marie," Pia said, her voice a whisper. "What is this place?"

"It's where the truth of who we are lies hidden," Marie replied, her voice calm but firm. She glanced back at Pia, her dark eyes glinting with a mix of reassurance and warning. "You may see things that will frighten you. That's natural. But understand this—you are safer here than anywhere else."

---

1. **Book Soundtrack Cue:** "Warriors" - Imagine Dragons.

Pia swallowed hard and nodded, though the unease prickling at the back of her neck didn't subside. She followed Marie as they moved further down the corridor. The air felt heavier, and the faint hum of energy seemed to vibrate through the stone walls.

Pia's fingertips tingled. The low torchlight suddenly seemed too bright. The sound of dripping water thundered in her ears. Something inside her was stirring—awakening.

Each door they passed seemed more imposing than the last, the carvings on them growing darker and more complex. One door was marked with jagged claw marks; another appeared to have molten gold seeping from its seams. Pia's heart raced as her imagination conjured what might lie behind them.

At last, they reached the end of the hall. The door here was the largest of all, towering nearly to the ceiling. It was carved from a dark wood that seemed to absorb the light from the torches. Runes etched in silver glimmered faintly, their patterns dizzying and unfamiliar.

Marie pulled an ancient-looking key from her nightgown, its metal tarnished but sturdy. She slipped it into the lock, and a deep, resonant *click* echoed through the hallway.

"Stay close," Marie murmured as she pushed the door open.

Pia stepped forward hesitantly, her breath catching in her throat. Beyond the door was not the enclosed chamber she had expected, but an open expanse. The night sky stretched above her, glittering with stars that seemed unnaturally bright. The air was cool and fresh, carrying the sound of a stream bubbling somewhere nearby.

As she stepped further into the room, Pia suddenly staggered as a gust of wind rushed past her, almost knocking her off balance. The sound of wings—massive, powerful wings—filled the air, their beats reverberating in her chest.

"Marie..." Pia whispered, gripping the older woman's arm.

"Be still," Marie said softly, her gaze fixed ahead. "And open your eyes."

Pia squinted, her vision adjusting to the dim light. At first, she saw only shadows—massive shapes that seemed to blend into the darkness. But then, two glowing blue eyes pierced through the gloom, locking onto her. Her stomach dropped, and her knees wobbled, but she stood her ground.

The creature stepped forward, its enormous body half-hidden by the shadows. The gleam of its scales caught the moonlight, and its sheer size dwarfed anything Pia had ever imagined. The air felt charged with an ancient power.

"What is it?" Pia breathed, her voice trembling.

Marie smiled faintly, her eyes gleaming with something between pride and awe. "This is what we strive for. The final stage of a

Nuru. You are closer to this than you think, Pia. Closer than most ever come."

The blue eyes narrowed slightly, and a low, rumbling growl echoed through the chamber. Pia's heart raced, but she couldn't look away. She wasn't sure if the creature was judging her, threatening her, or simply seeing her—but whatever it was, she felt stripped bare, as if it could peer into the deepest parts of her soul.

Marie turned to Pia. She waved her hand and illuminated the area. Before her, more than a dozen dragons stood in a semicircle, their massive forms glowing faintly in the starlight. Each dragon was unique—some with shimmering golden scales that reflected the light like divine light fire, others with deep obsidian hides that seemed to drink in the darkness around them. A few glowed faintly with hues of blue or green, their forms exuding an ethereal radiance.

Pia's knees nearly buckled. Her breath came in short gasps, and she instinctively pressed a hand to her chest, as if to steady the rapid pounding of her heart. Their eyes—sapphire, violet, emerald, and ruby—were all fixed on her, unblinking and intense. The air was thick with their power, a pulsing energy that seemed to hum in her very bones.

She took a shaky step forward, her senses overwhelmed by the sheer majesty of the creatures before her. Their scales glimmered like treasure hoards, their wings stretching wide before folding in regal poses. One dragon, with silver scales streaked with gold, tilted its massive head, regarding her with what seemed like curiosity.

"They're…" Pia started, her voice trailing off. She didn't have the words to capture what she felt—fear, awe, wonder. The dragons radiated power, but there was something else there too, something ancient and knowing.

"They sense your potential," Marie said, her tone softer now. "Dragons do not see the way we do. They see who you are, who you were, and who you may become—all at once. They see your soul."

Pia shivered as one of the dragons, a hulking black figure with glowing blue eyes, stepped forward. Its movements were slow, deliberate, and graceful despite its size. A low rumble echoed in its chest, and for a moment, Pia feared it would strike.

Instead, it lowered its head slightly, as though bowing. The gesture sent a ripple of shock through her, and she glanced at Marie, who smiled faintly.

Pia glanced at Marie, who stood so still, the dragons didn't seem to notice her. Or maybe they did—and respected her more than they feared her.

"They honor you," Marie said. "They know what you are becoming."

Pia felt tears prick at the corners of her eyes. She didn't feel ready, didn't feel worthy of their gaze, let alone their respect. But as she stood there, surrounded by beings of unfathomable power, a new feeling began to bloom in her chest—a sense of belonging, of destiny, of hope.

"They're also restless, Pia," Ms. Marie added.

"Restless?" Pia questioned.

"Yes, because they know what is to come," Ms. Marie said with a sigh.

"What's that?" Pia asked.

"War."

Pia looked at the dragons once more—no longer with fear, but with fire in her chest. If war was coming, she wouldn't face it alone.

ABOUT THE AUTHOR

Nie Harvey is the pen name of M.P. Sudduth—when she's not coaching entrepreneurs, building brands, or raising her tribe, she's telling raw stories that make readers feel seen. Nie writes for the bold, the faith-driven, and the visionaries who refuse to be boxed in. Her work is a collision of creativity, conviction, and a little rebellion—whether she's talking about faith, identity, or the messiness of purpose.

With roots in Mississippi and a heart for generational impact, Nie writes to ignite legacy and stir something eternal. She believes you were born to disrupt the ordinary—and Nie Harvey is the unapologetic proof.

When she's not writing under Nie Harvey, M.P. Sudduth is a multi-passionate educator, business coach, and the powerhouse behind MPowering Legacy Publishing, who writes inspirational business books such as *My Wine, My Wilderness, Stepping Into Your Legacy,* and *God-Made CEO.*

Follow Nie's fearless pen on <u>Facebook</u> or connect through autho rnieharvey@gmail.com.

SNEAK PEEK OF BOOK 2

THE EDGE OF WINDSORVILLE

C hapter One

    The music began, a beautiful mix of African drums and "La Marcha", harmonizing in a way that felt almost magical as Rosa walked down the aisle. Ms. Marie, seated near the front, was the picture of elegance. Her long, natural gray hair cascaded over her shoulders, and her soft lavender dress complemented her radiant smile. She dabbed her eyes with a handkerchief as the ceremony commenced.

Tay sat next to Ms. Marie, looking sharp in a perfectly tailored suit that accentuated his deep, dark brown waves. He tapped his feet to the music, swaying to and fro with a serene look on his face. Next to him sat Zaya, who looked stunning in a flowy chiffon gown the color of twilight. Her braids were adorned with delicate silver thread. She sat with her grandfather, who wore a deep blue tux. Mr. Wright was proud to witness this union, as he knew the pain that Claire's death caused Pierre.

Near Zaya were Yazen and Yazmeen. The twins, who lived two counties over, were friends of Zaya. They had hung out with Pia and Abel a few times and were invited to the wedding. Yazen and Yazmeen were dressed to impress. Yazen wore a sleek black suit with a deep emerald green tie and matching pocket square, his polished shoes gleaming under the soft light. His locs were styled neatly, and his quiet confidence added to his charm. Yazmeen complemented him perfectly in a flowing emerald green gown with gold embroidery along the neckline and hem. Her locs were styled in an intricate updo, adorned with small gold pins that sparkled as she moved. Together, the twins were a striking pair, their attire adding another layer of elegance to the event.

The sun hung low in the sky, casting a golden hue over the lush garden where Pierre and Rosa's wedding was about to take place. The sun hung low in the sky, casting a golden hue over the lush garden where Pierre and Rosa's wedding was about to take place.

Rosa stood across from Pierre, radiant in a gown of ivory lace that flowed like water. Her veil, adorned with tiny crystals, shimmered in the sunlight. Her bouquet was a mix of calla lilies and vibrant sunflowers, tied together with a ribbon of gold. Pia, standing by her side as a bridesmaid, adjusted the hem of her flowy navy dress.

Pia's coils were adorned with golden beads, and her warm smile mirrored the joy of the occasion.

Abel, standing tall as one of Pierre's groomsmen, straightened his tie and clapped Pierre on the back. Abel, and his date, Amber, who sat in the audience, wore navy with gold accents. Pierre wore a tailored cream suit with a vibrant pocket square, blending seamlessly with the golden accents of the decor. His salt and pepper barbershop fade nicely trimmed his almond brown eyes, which glistened with joy.

It had been three months since Pierre and Rosa's engagement announcement, and once the internet was restored, the two decided not to wait to have their ceremony. The summer months passed by quickly as schools adjusted their schedule to get students back on track. Businesses were fluttered with customers who missed their convenient services, and lightning fast communication all over the world had picked up like it never left. Pierre and Rosa decided to keep both houses and take turns staying in each. Rosa, disappointed that Lilliana refused to attend the wedding, had begun to develop a bond with Pia and enjoyed her company. The couple decided on a late September wedding, eager to tie the knot.

Pia was entering her final year at school and would graduate with a Bachelor of Fine Arts in the spring, along with Zaya, who would finish with a Political Science degree and head to law school and Abel, who would finish with an MBA. Their lives seemed to be back on track and flourishing. Pia also grew very fond of Yazen and the feeling was mutual. Yet, she felt she knew her fate would keep them apart, so she kept their friendship at surface level. She also did not want to risk another heartbreak, as she thought of Nolan often.

Pia also spent the summer learning how to harness her powers. She felt strong and in control. Abel kept her secret, which allowed them to grow closer. He was aware of Ms. Marie and the dragons, although he had never been allowed to meet them.

While everything seemed to be going well, no one could figure out a way to delete ThermaTrace. The app did not do anything, as far as anyone knew—no notifications, no activity, no in-app purchases. It was just there, an orange icon with one T. The Nurus had their suspicions, but nothing was concrete.

Just as Pierre began his vows, a low hum filled the air, growing louder by the second. The crowd stirred uneasily, looking toward the horizon. Suddenly, military drones appeared overhead, casting shadows over the vibrant decorations. A convoy of armored vehicles rolled into the garden, the ground trembling beneath their weight. Soldiers in dark uniforms and visors fanned out, weapons pointed at the guests.

"This is a government operation. We are here under direct orders to locate Pia Pierce and Rhema Marie Brown. Everyone remain where you are," the commanding officer said after stepping forward.

Pierre instinctively stepped in front of Pia, shielding her, while Abel positioned himself protectively near Ms. Marie. Ms. Marie's serene expression hardened as she rose from her seat, her long gray hair catching the light. "What is the meaning of this?" she demanded, her voice steady but laced with authority.

"Marie Brown," the officer said, stepping closer. "We have reason to believe you and Pia are in possession of information critical to national security. You will come with us now."

Pia's eyes darted around the garden, searching for an escape. "I'm not going anywhere," she said defiantly, her hands clenched into fists.

"You'll have no choice," the officer snapped, signaling to his troops. The soldiers began advancing, their boots crunching on the gravel paths.

"This is a wedding, not a battlefield! Have some respect! You do not have permission to take my daughter anywhere!" Pierre said, his deep voice cutting through the chaos.

"Unfortunately, Mr. Pierce, we do not need your permission. She's coming with us."

The tension in the air was electric. Rosa clung to Pierre, tears welling in her eyes as their perfect day spiraled into a nightmare. Zaya moved to shield a group of children nearby, her gown flowing like a protective curtain.

Ms. Marie raised her hand, commanding silence. "If you've come for me, leave everyone else out of this. Let the couple have their day." Her gaze was fierce, unyielding.

"No!" Pia yelled, her eyes looking at Ms. Marie in terror.

The officer hesitated, but a soldier spoke into his earpiece. Moments later, the drones withdrew slightly, though the soldiers remained on high alert. "You have five minutes to comply," the officer said grimly.

A deafening roar tore through the air. Shadows shifted over the garden, and all eyes turned skyward. Gasps of awe and terror echoed as a massive dragon soared overhead, its shimmering scales catching the fading sunlight. Its wings beat powerfully, sending gusts of wind rippling through the garden, causing flowers to sway and decorations to flutter wildly.

The dragon's presence was majestic and overwhelming, its golden eyes scanning the scene below as though observing. For a moment, it hovered, exuding an aura of sheer power.

Everyone gasped and crouched down in fear. Dragons had been spotted all over the country, but not one had been seen publicly in Windsorville.

"Target acquired!" barked a soldier into his comms. The drones immediately shifted their attention to the dragon. They whirred into action, zipping upward to encircle the historic creature.

"Focus on the aerial threat!" the commanding officer shouted, signaling a group of soldiers to break away and head toward their vehicles. Armed personnel scrambled to respond, their attention completely diverted from the wedding party.

The dragon released another ear-splitting roar, but it didn't attack. Instead, it ascended higher, wings slicing through the sky with startling precision. The drones pursued, their small forms like gnats against the massive beast, while several soldiers piled into armored vehicles, engines roaring to life as they raced after the dragon.

Pia exhaled shakily, her fists unclenching. "It's a distraction," she whispered to Abel, who nodded grimly. Ms. Marie's sharp eyes followed the dragon's path before flicking back to the scattered soldiers. "We don't have much time," she murmured, her voice low but resolute.

The remaining soldiers were fewer now, their formation loosened by the sudden shift in focus. The dragon's unexpected arrival had temporarily shifted the balance of power.

"Abel," Ms. Marie whispered. "I need ya to promise me something."

"Anything," Abel responded.

"No matter what happens here. Take care of Tay. Get him home!" Marie said sternly.

A group of soldiers marched forward, breaking through the wedding party. Two grabbed Ms. Marie by the arms, forcing her down despite her dignified resistance.

"Get your hands off her!" Abel shouted, stepping forward, but was pushed back by the butt of a rifle. Pia grabbed his arm, holding him steady as anger flashed in her eyes. She could sense Tay's energy surging, and feared what would happen if they knew he had powers, too.

Two more soldiers advanced on Pia. Abel stepped in their path, his stance protective, but one swung his weapon at him, knocking him to the ground. Pia let out a cry as they seized her arms. The air around her seemed to ripple, a faint glow emanating from her skin.

"What are you doing?!" Rosa screamed, clutching Pierre. The ceremony was in shambles, guests scattering and crying out in fear.

Ms. Marie, now in cuffs, was pulled to her feet. Her eyes locked with Pia's, a silent message passing between them. "Don't," she mouthed, but Pia's expression hardened.

The ripple around Pia intensified, her body trembling as the glow grew brighter. "Let her go!" she shouted, her voice echoing unnaturally. A pulse of fire burst from her, knocking the soldiers holding her to the ground. The force sent nearby decorations flying and caused everyone to stumble.

Pierre's eyes widened as he stared at his daughter. "Pia..." he whispered, his voice a mix of shock and awe.

The remaining soldiers froze, their weapons trained on her, unsure of their next move. Ms. Marie, though restrained, smiled faintly, pride and sadness mingling in her expression. The dragon's roar echoed in the distance, as though heralding the beginning of something extraordinary—something unstoppable.